P9-CAU-380

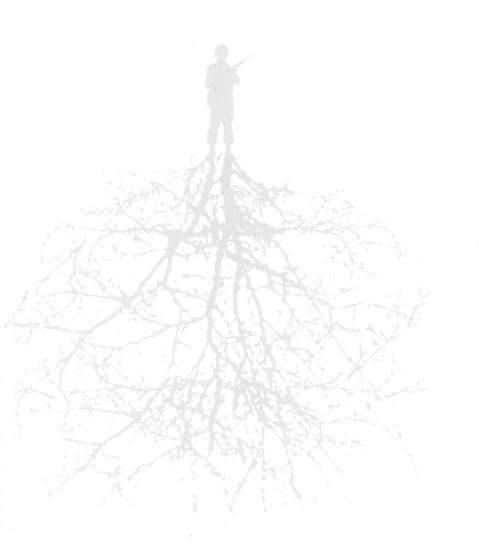

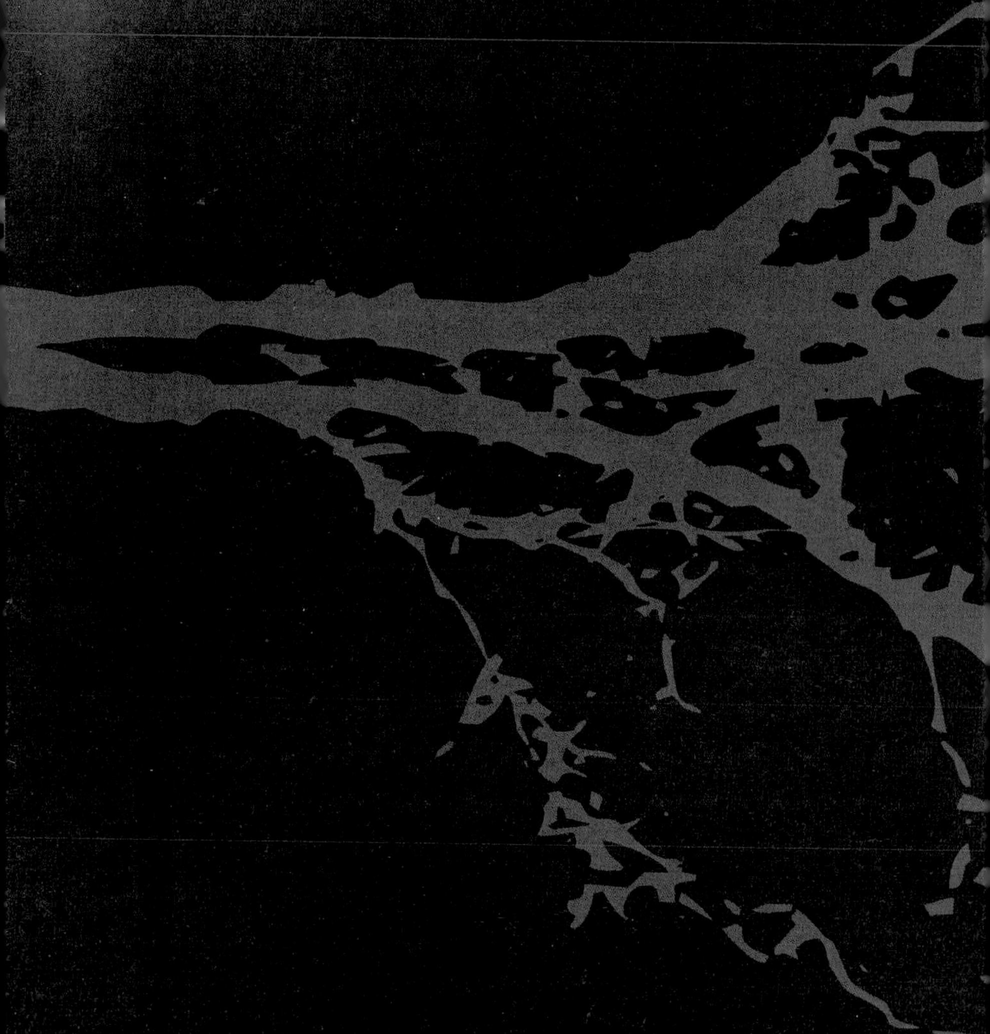

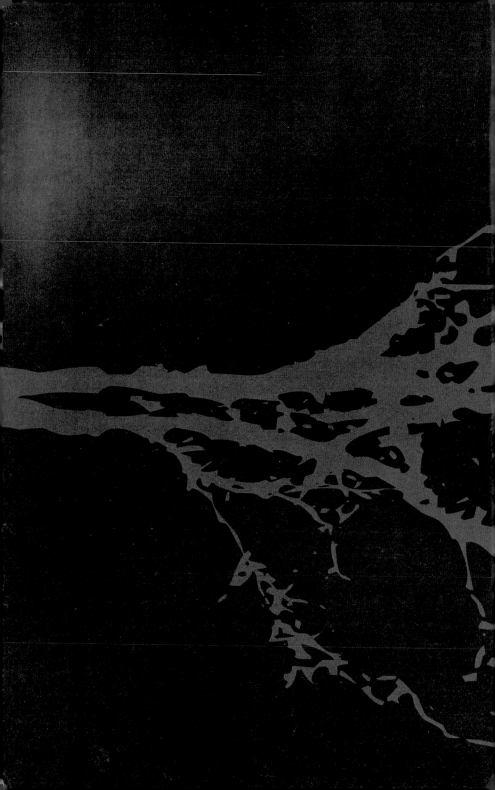

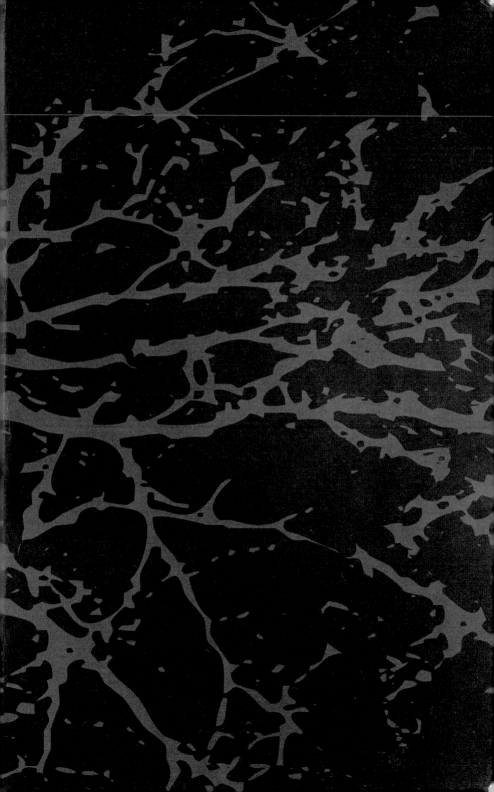

BLOODLINES

BLOOD BROTHERHOOD

written by
M. Zachary Sherman

illustrated by
Fritz Casas

colored by
Marlon Ilagan

STONE ARCH BOOKS
a capstone imprint

DEDICATED TO THE MEN AND WOMEN
OF THE ARMED SERVICES

Bloodlines is published by Stone Arch Books, A
Capstone Imprint, 151 Good Counsel Drive, P.O. Box
669 Mankato, Minnesota 56002 www.capstonepub.
com Copyright © 2011 by Stone Arch Books All
rights reserved. No part of this publication may
be reproduced in whole or in part, or stored in a
retrieval system, or transmitted in any form or by
any means, electronic, mechanical, photocopying,
recording, or otherwise, without written permission
of the publisher.

Cataloging-in-Publication Data is available on the
Library of Congress website.
ISBN: 978-1-4342-2559-7 (library binding)
ISBN: 978-1-4342-3098-0 (paperback)

Summary: On December 1, 1950, during the heart
of the Korean War, Lieutenant Everett Donovan
awakens in a mortar crater behind enemy lines.
During the Battle of Chosin Reservoir, a mine
explosion has killed his entire platoon of U.S.
Marines. Shaken and shivering from the subzero
temps, the lieutenant struggles to his feet and
stands among the bodies of his fellow Devil Dogs.
Suddenly, a shot rings out! Donovan falls to his
knees and when he looks up, he's face to face
with his Korean counterpart. Both men know the
standoff will end in brotherhood or blood — and
neither choice will come easy.

Art Director: Bob Lentz
Graphic Designer: Brann Garvey
Production Specialist: Michelle Biedscheid

Photo credits: Corbis: Bettmann, 48; Corel, 35;
Department of Defense photo, 49; Getty Images
Inc.: AFP/STR, 34, Archive Photos/Bachrach, 19,
Central Press, 81, Picture Post/Bert Hardy, 19, Three
Lions, 7, Time Life Pictures/National Archives,
18, Time Life Pictures/National Archives/Frank
C. Kerr, 68; U.S. Marine Corps photo by Corporal
Peter McDonald, 67, Cpl. W.T. Wolfe, 80; Wikipedia:
Antique Military Rifles, 35

Printed in the United States of America
in Stevens Point, Wisconsin
092010   005934WZS11

TABLE OF CONTENTS

PERSONNEL FILE

Captain
Everett Donovan

ORGANIZATION:
1st Marine Division, 3rd Battalion,
5th Marine Regiment

ENTERED SERVICE AT:
Camp Pendleton, CA

BORN:
March 25, 1932

EQUIPMENT

M1951 Winter Helmet

M1951 Field Jacket

M1951 Pistol Belt

Ammunition

M2 Garand

First-Aid Pouch

.45 Caliber Pistol

Combat Boots

OVERVIEW: KOREAN WAR

For thousands of years, people have fought over Korea. From 1910 until the end of World War II, Japan controlled the entire peninsula. However, after the war, Korea was divided into two parts. Russia controlled the northern half of the peninsula, and the United States controlled the southern half. Three years later, the two halves became independent nations — North Korea and South Korea. But their troubles were just beginning. On June 25, 1950, North Korea, led by their communist ruler Kim Il Sung, attacked the South. This action started what would become the Korean War.

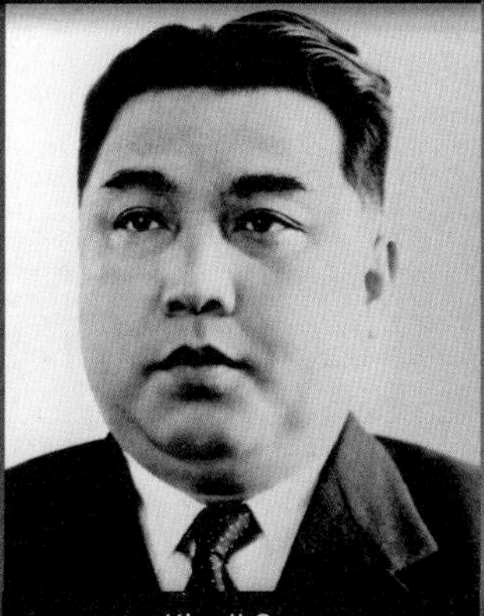

Kim Il Sung

MAP

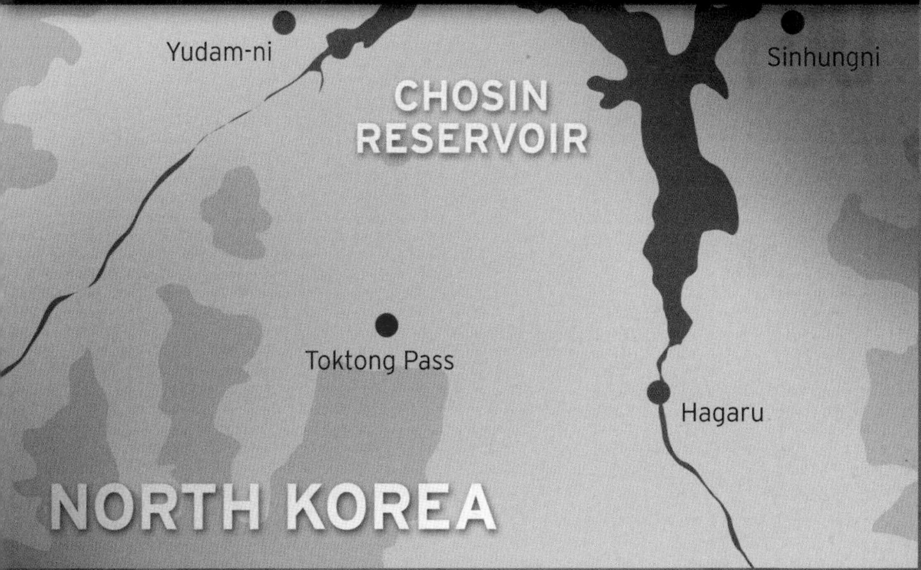
Yudam-ni
Sinhungni
CHOSIN RESERVOIR
Toktong Pass
Hagaru
NORTH KOREA

MISSION

Scout an area known as the Toktong Pass and provide security for UN and U.S. military forces to advance through this enemy-occupied territory.

CHAPTER 001

OUT OF FOCUS

Sunlight.

Golden rays stabbed at the back of the man's brain as his eyes fluttered open. The world around him was hazy and out of focus. A muffled humming filled his ears, deafening his surroundings as he tried to sit up. His head felt like he was balancing a bowling ball on his neck. His own shallow breathing echoed in his skull.

Blinking, he tried to focus. The landscape surrounding him became clearer. Where was he? What was going on?

His eyes scanned over a filthy M2 carbine rifle still clutched in his hands. Its bolt was open and the ammo magazine was empty. His M1951 Cold Weather Uniform was caked in frozen mud and covered with snow. His hands, though dirty and bruised, were both still there and seemed to work okay. He used one of them to shield his pain-filled eyes from the sunbeams radiating down on him.

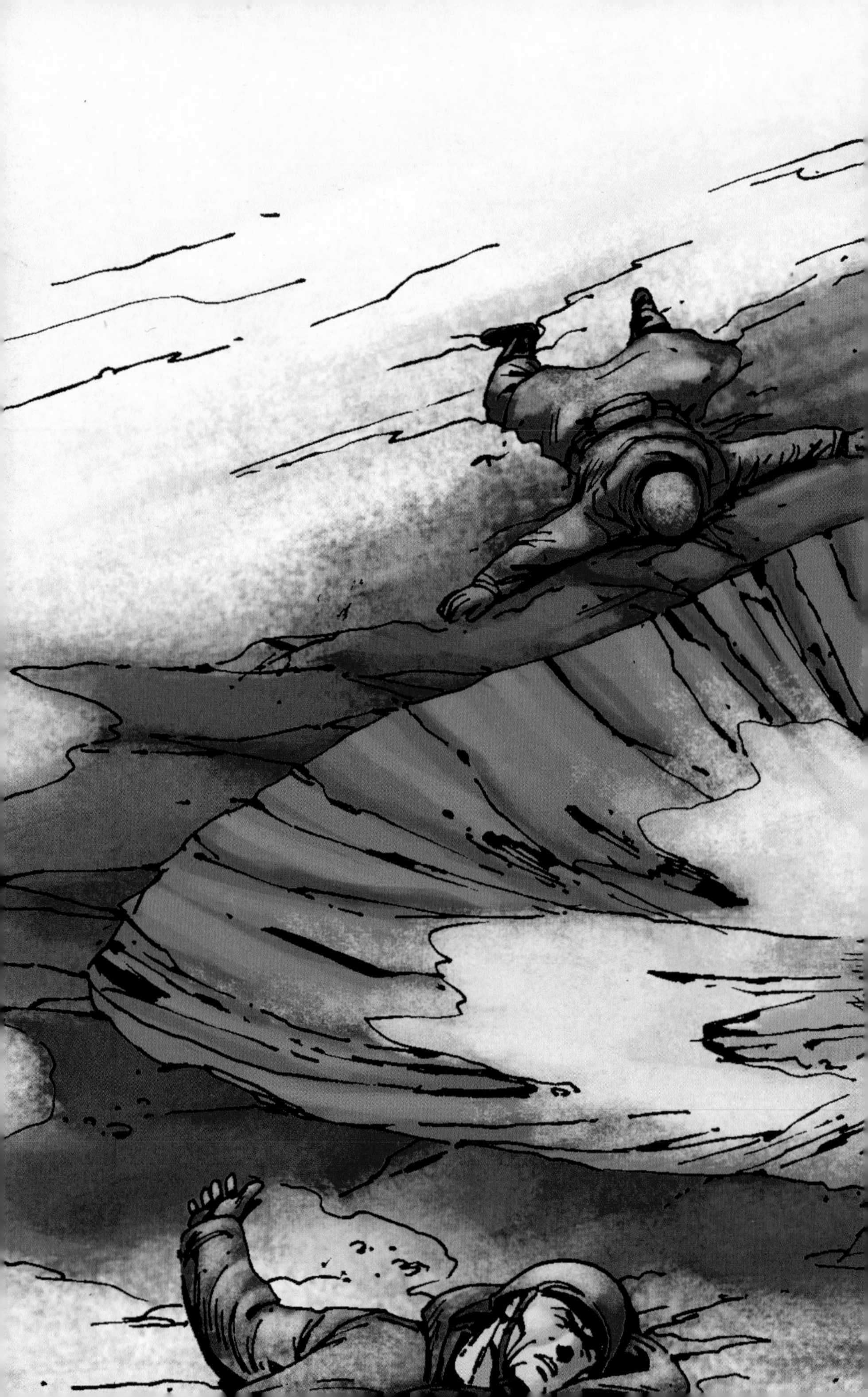

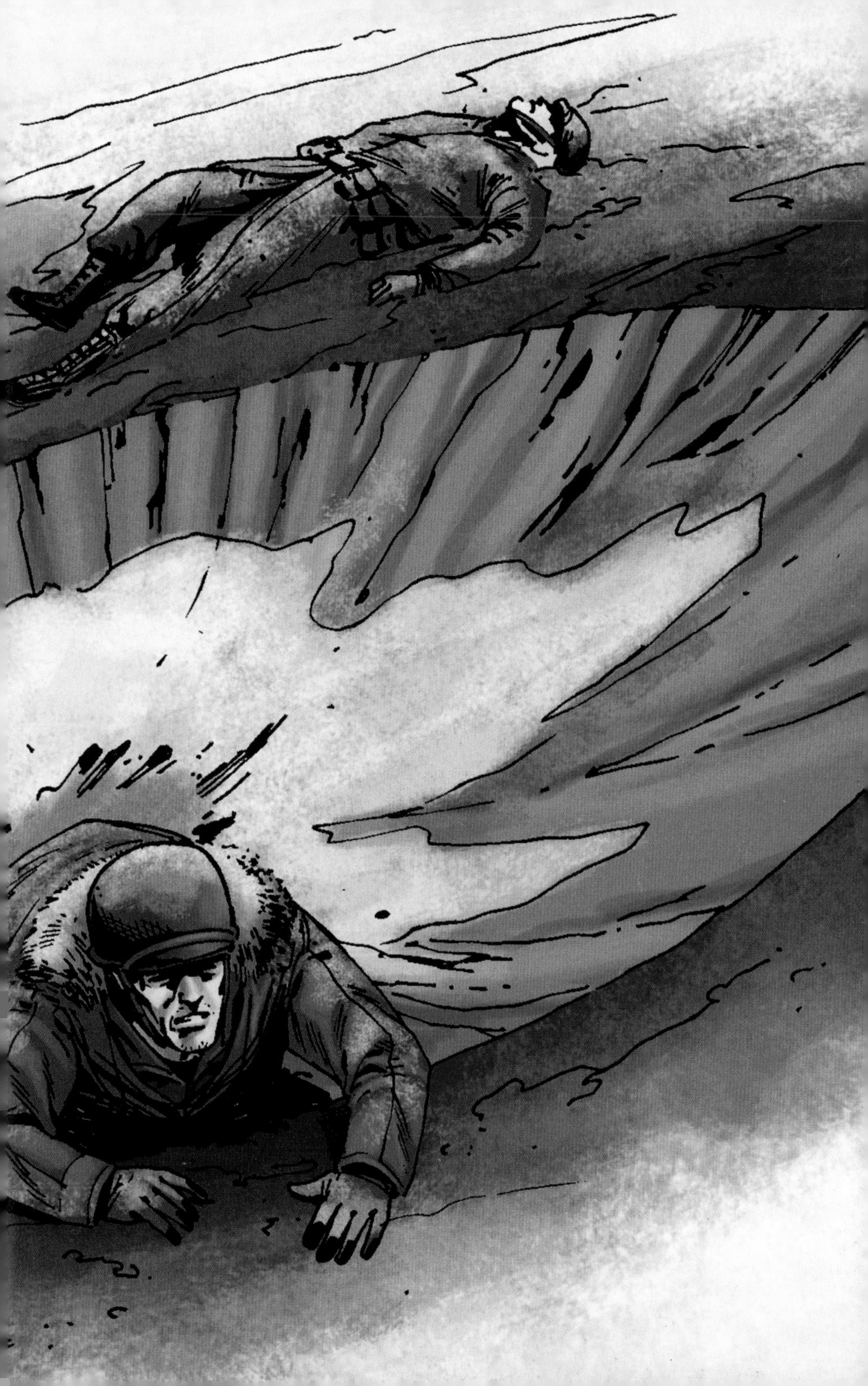

Getting to his knees, the soldier noticed something odd. He was standing in a medium-sized mortar crater. Fragments of the charred metal casings scattered about told that tale, but they were all covered in new snow. It was clear that whatever had happened hadn't been a recent event. He'd been unconscious for some time.

Desperately, the soldier tried to remember the events of the day. Every time he reached back into that part of his memory, all he could muster were flashes of white-hot light that made his skull ache. He shook the cobwebs from his head as his vision became locked-on and solid.

Obviously, he thought, *I've been out for a while. Time to figure out where I am.*

Standing now, he looked over the edge of the earthly depression. What he saw made his blood run cold.

Blast craters. Spent ammo shells. Scorched earth. Smoldering trees. And between all of that lay the bodies of twenty dead United States Marines. Lifeless, they sank in a veil of freshly fallen snow.

Clearly, a battle had taken place here. And they had certainly lost.

By the look of things, Captain Everett Donovan, 1st Marine Division, 3rd Battalion, 5th Marine Regiment, was lucky to be alive.

Coming out of the crater, he looked over what was left of his men. He was the captain in charge of these Marines, and they were just that — his. His team of Counterintelligence Marines. His responsibility. And this? This was *his* failure. At least that's how he felt, though he knew that wasn't really true.

Tears welled up in his swollen eyes as he surveyed the bodies. Donovan tried desperately to remember what had happened here, but nothing, not even a single image, came back to him. All he knew was that these men were gone, and somehow he'd survived.

Captain Donovan gnashed his teeth. He walked from one fallen Marine to the next. He removed their dog tags and searched the bodies for personal items like death letters that would be sent to loved ones in case they didn't make it home. He felt like a sick vulture as he knelt over them, rummaging through their pockets. A little part of him died every time he went through a fallen Marine's pouch.

Coming upon his radio operator, Donovan reached for the field radio, but it was punched full of bullet holes.

Well, that's not going to work, he thought.

Donovan looked at his watch. He tried to estimate how long he'd been out. "Dang!" he said softly, examining the face. "I just got this fixed." The watch was cracked, just like it had been when his brother gave it to him before he'd deployed.

"Dad would've wanted you to have this. It kept me safe in Europe, and I'm sure it'll do the same for you in Korea," he remembered his brother Mike saying. Though the glass was cracked, the gears were still going strong. The watch still kept perfect time.

"Just like a Donovan," Everett had replied with a grin.

"Like a Donovan, for sure," Mike had answered.

But no, he wasn't back home with his brother. He was stuck on the frozen tundra of the Chosin Reservoir in North Korea, fighting in conditions never faced by soldiers. He wondered how he'd even gotten here, especially after just fighting a war in the Pacific.

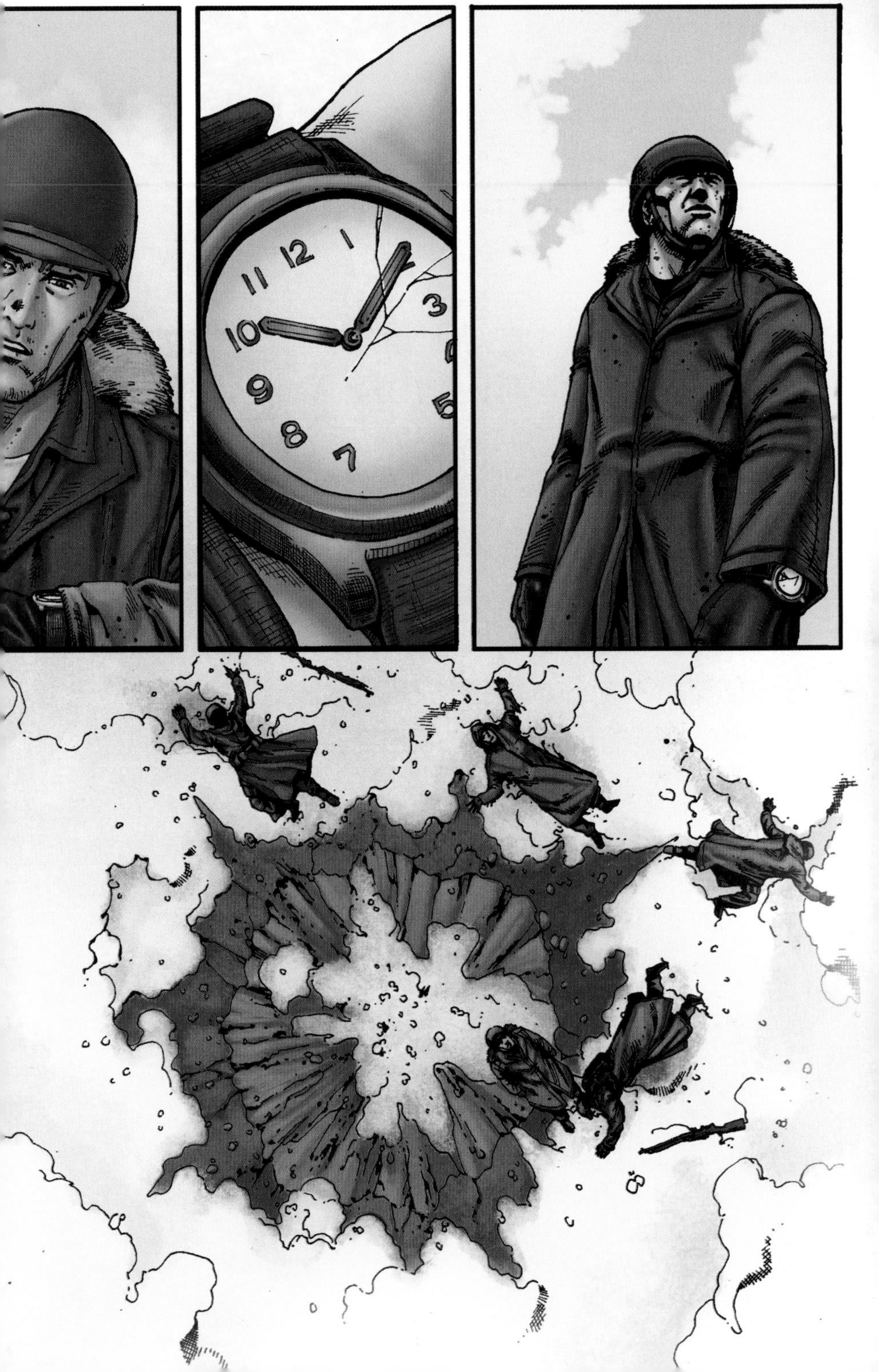

But the reasons didn't matter now as he squatted down and unfolded his map. Using his compass, he was able to zero his location and plot a route to the Marine Forward Observation Base. It was hard to know if they'd still be there. He didn't even know what day it was. Because of the freshly fallen flurries, and since extreme cold slowed body decomposition, checking bodies wasn't going to help figure out the date either.

It was 35 degrees below zero and getting colder as the sun started to dip in the sky. He needed to move. It was a five-hour trek to the base, but that'd turn into an entire day's journey, easily. Thanks to everything from long cliff drops to enemy land mines between him and the base — not to mention the entire Korean army — he'd have to take it slow. And since their Chinese allies had a reputation for not treating prisoners of war too kindly, the last thing he wanted was to be captured.

Suddenly, a light snow began to fall. Donovan slung his rifle over one shoulder and his bag of supplies over the other. After taking one last look at his men, he tilted his helmet to his fallen friends and set out across the frozen Toktong Pass.

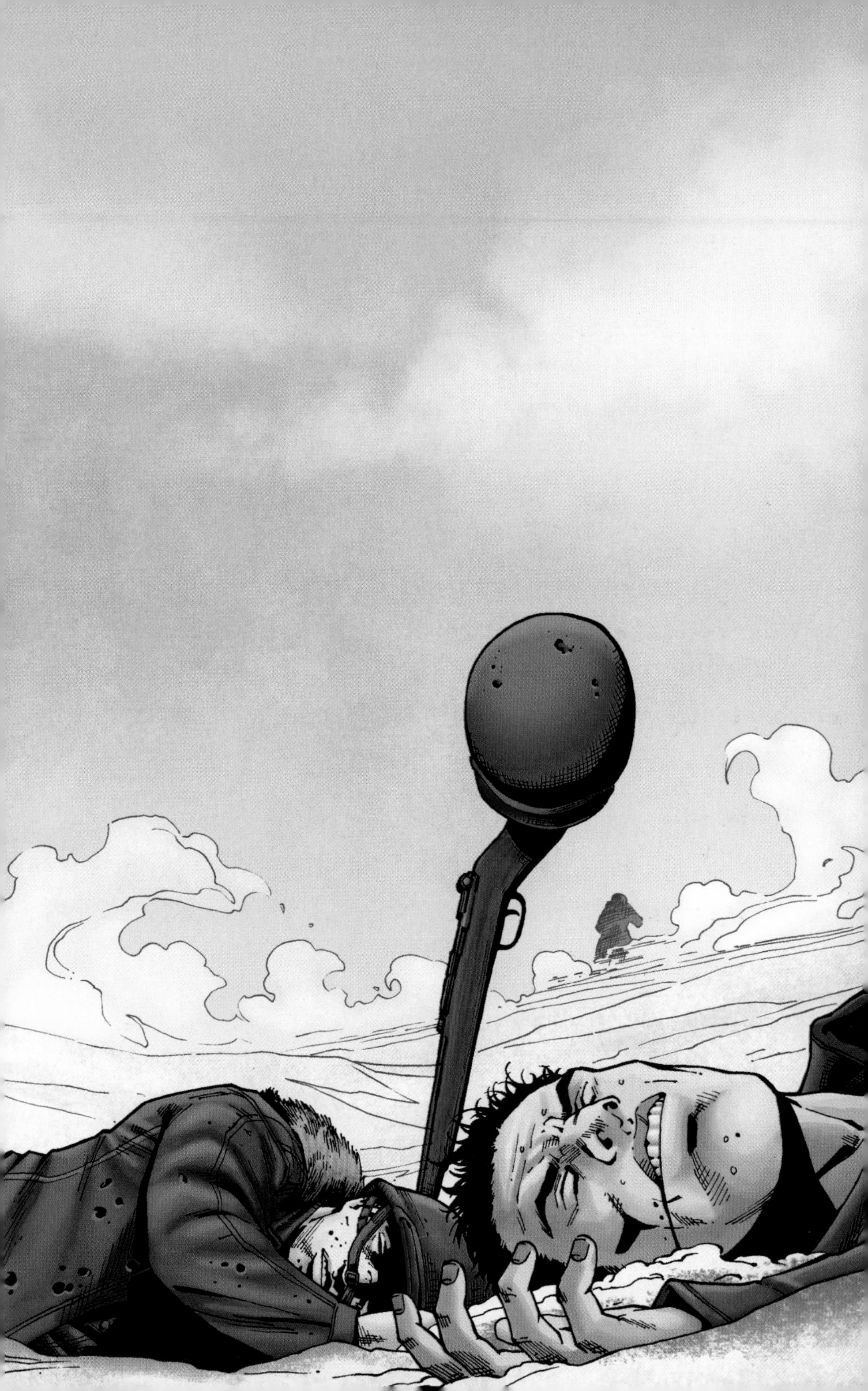

DEBRIEFING

38TH PARALLEL

YOU ARE NOW CROSSING
38TH PARALLEL
US CO.B 728MP

HISTORY

Just days before the end of World War II, the Russian army entered Korea, which had been occupied by Japan. In an effort to stop their advancement, the U.S. War Department set the 38th parallel as a dividing line between the northern and southern half of the Korean Peninsula. In 1950, the Russian-backed North Korean army attacked the south. The South Korean army, along with their U.S. allies, tried to stop them during three years of battles. Today, the 38th parallel still divides North and South Korea – as well as the ideas of communism and democracy.

QUICK FACTS

– The 38th parallel was first suggested as a dividing line as early as 1896.

– Neither North or South Korea approved the original demarcation line. It was established by the U.S. War Department.

– After the Korean War, the 38th parallel became known as the Demilitarized Zone (DMZ). This middle ground still separates the two countries.

– The DMZ stretches 162 miles across the Korean Peninsula. It is nearly 2.5 miles wide.

U.S. TROOPS IN KOREA

HISTORY

When North Korea invaded South Korea on June 25, 1950, U.S. President Harry Truman spoke with his Joint Chief of Staff, Omar Bradley. Truman and Bradley agreed to "draw the line" on the advancement of communist governments like Russia and North Korea. On June 27, they committed air and naval support and promised U.S. troops as part of an "international peacekeeping force." During the next three years, more than 5.7 million U.S. soldiers would serve as part of the mission to keep North Korea on their side of the 38th parallel.

OMAR BRADLEY

Omar N. Bradley (1893-1981) served as the first chairman of the U.S. Joint Chiefs of Staff.

CHAPTER 002

NEVER STOP MOVING

Donovan had to stop himself from whistling as he continued his lonely trek through the snow. He tried to take his mind off the cold and the wetness, but melted snow soaked through his double-buckle combat boots and deep into his woolly socks. Whistling was a nervous habit he'd picked up at boot camp and one that'd landed him in trouble every time he was caught doing it. Every sergeant instructor that called him on it made him write essay after essay on "the merits of Noise Discipline and the reasons we have it."

The thought made him chuckle as he pressed through the trees, heading deeper into the Toktong Pass. Finally, he came to a small clearing in the forest and stopped. Crouching, he scanned the open grove cautiously. It was like a small baseball field with tree lines on either side. The forest made great cover, but it would be a more roundabout way home and a harder path to travel.

The forest was not impossible, but Captain Donovan was extremely worried about land mines. The enemy would certainly have placed mines in there, knowing a person would fear the openness of the grove and would probably try to go around.

Looking at his map again, Donovan knew it was a guessing game, one he could go back and forth with for hours. Safe or not, it didn't matter. Straight through the open field was the fastest way, period.

Donovan looked up again and sighed. He unslung his weapon, chambered a round, and began slowly walking through the grove. The Marine was on high alert.

About fifteen yards in, Donovan noticed the true beauty of his surroundings.

Untouched snow blanketed everything in shades of white for as far as the eye could see. He marveled at how tree limbs were so used to the snowfall's weight, they dipped but didn't break. It was like something out of a Christmas painting.

As moments past, Donovan almost forgot he was in a combat situation . . . almost.

BANG!

Donovan's right shoulder suddenly jerked hard to the rear. His confusion was immediately replaced by intense pain that crashed over him. Waves of blood emerged from the new hole in his upper arm. It splattered red, contrasting sharply against the soft whiteness of snow blanketing the ground.

As his right arm flew backward, his rifle spun end over end out of his hand. Finally, it landed about five yards away from him. Donovan's feet corkscrewed under him, causing him to fall immediately to the ground with a loud thud.

Donovan had been shot by a sniper's bullet.

Gritting his teeth, he placed a hand on the wound. The bullet was lodged deep in the shoulder, but it was in the muscle. That meant the wound wasn't life threatening yet, but blood loss and immediate infection would become a major factor — and fast. He scrambled for his sidearm, pulling it free from the leather holster. Then he looked at his M2 rifle, half buried in the snow.

Reaching for his rifle, Donovan yanked his hand back just in time as another silenced shot impacted the snow.

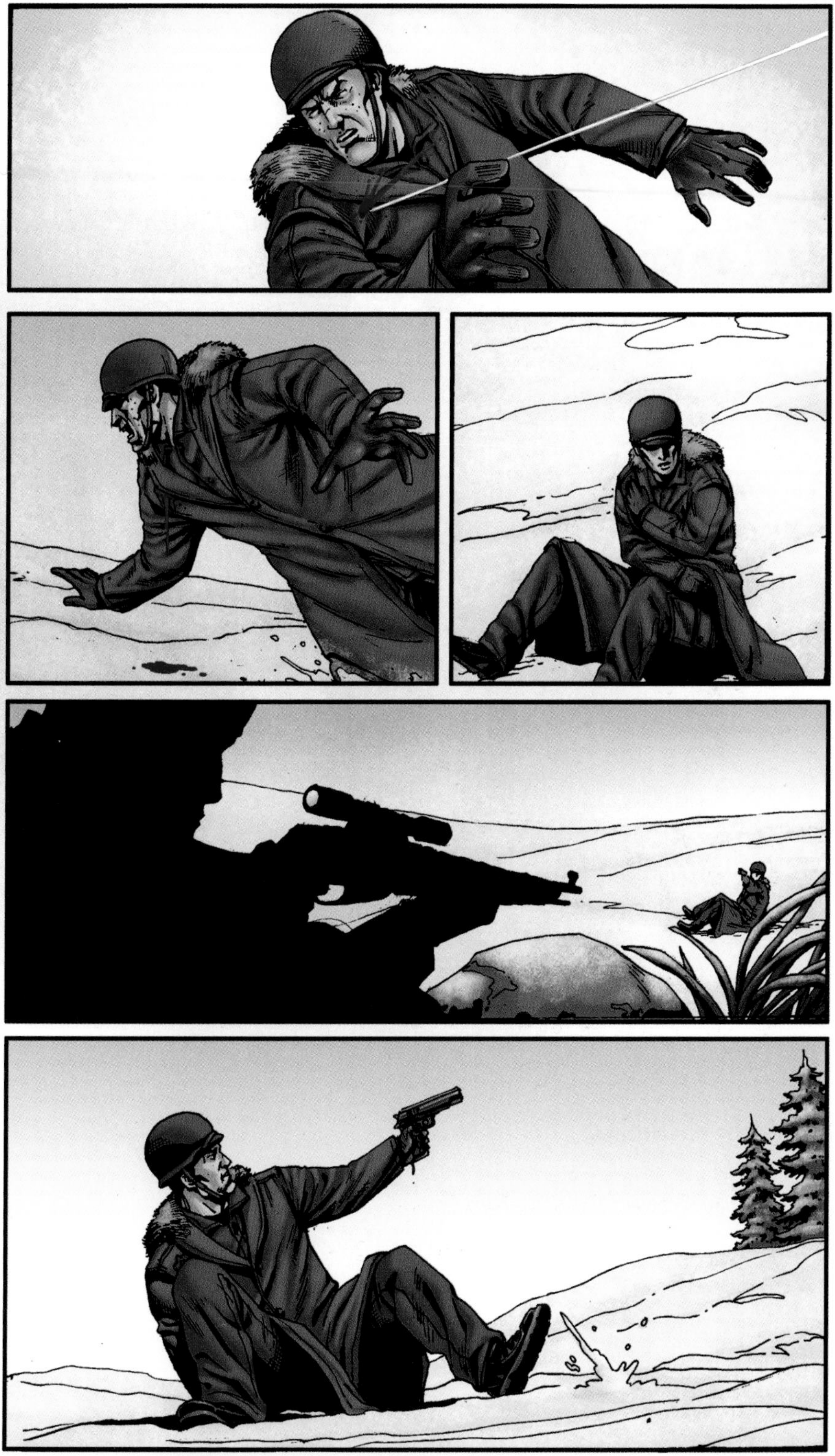

Out in the open, Everett Donovan was in a bad spot. He knew he needed to get to cover fast, or he was dead. Donovan quickly got to his feet, eyed his entry point to cover, and began running toward the trees.

Shots exploded from his .45 pistol as he ran.

BANG! BANG! BAN

Bullets pierced trees where he thought the sniper's location was, but he hit nothing.

As the tree line approached, he dove in, hit the ground with his good shoulder, and slid down a thirty-foot bank of frozen mud and snow. Finally sliding to a stop, Donovan shook off the pain. He raised his weapon. Nothing was in front of him. As he stood, the crunching of snow underfoot alerted him to someone behind.

With his pistol in the air, he stopped and opened his eyes wide. Pointed at his chest was the barrel of a Mosin-Nagant M91/30 sniper rifle with telescopic sight.

Holding onto the gun's hand grip was the biggest North Korean soldier Donovan had ever seen. He was five feet, ten inches tall, and 195 pounds of solid muscle. He was covered from head to toe in a light green uniform that had been bleached more white than green, thanks to the harsh elements. The jacket and pants were quilted for warmth, and Donovan wondered if this added to the man's bulk. Ammo pouches flapped open against the sniper's chest, revealing a well-stacked supply of lead. He wore a large bayonet on his belt.

This Korean was a killing machine, hands down.

Though his hand shook a bit, Donovan was still able to hold his pistol in the air. The captain had never been in a situation like this before, and no amount of training could ever prep a Marine for a gun-to-gun, point-blank stalemate with the enemy.

A moment passed before either of them did anything.

Donovan could feel the warm liquid flowing over his cold skin. Blood trickled down his arm, and the lightweight pistol began to grow heavy in his hand. As he fought to keep it in the air, Donovan grimaced slightly.

The Korean noticed.

And Donovan noticed the Korean noticing.

This made Donovan angry. He was a Marine and that meant he wasn't typically allowed to show weakness. But the events of the day were anything but typical.

"Funny, isn't it?" Donovan said with smile. "Two soldiers trained to kill the enemy at all costs, and neither one of us is willing to risk their own life to do it. Wonder if this is in a field manual somewhere?"

Donovan chuckled. Then he recoiled in pain as the jarring from his laughter caused his shoulder to flame up.

Slowly, Donovan backed up a couple of paces, as did the Korean sniper. Finally, Donovan sat on a log, and the Korean sat on a broken tree stump. Neither one of them lowered their weapons.

Slumping on a tree, Donovan used his left hand to reach for his canteen. It wasn't there. He looked around, but he couldn't see it anywhere.

"Great. Not only am I gonna to die, I'm gonna die thirsty," Donovan said.

He cursed himself as he suddenly heard a sloshing in a metal receptacle in front of him.

Looking up, he saw the Korean swigging a long drink of water from Donovan's own canteen.

"Son of a —! Where did you get that!?" He groaned as pain filled his arm again, and he grabbed his muscle. The world began getting darker. Blood loss was beginning to make him woozy.

"It was a stupid mistake, you know?" Donovan said.

The Korean soldier's eyes narrowed.

"It's the first thing they teach you," Donovan continued. "Keep moving under fire. Don't stop when the shooting starts — even if you're hit."

The Korean drank out of the metal canteen again. He appeared to listen to the American carry on. The way the sniper stared, the Korean almost seemed to understand Donovan's ranting.

"It's the hardest thing for a Marine to learn," Donovan explained. "Instinct makes you wanna hug the dirt, but something inside keeps yelling 'Move.' Finally you do, and you just hope it's in the right direction."

Glistening tears began to well up in his eyes. Donovan looked around, not sure what to do.

"This country is absolutely the most beautiful place I've ever seen," he said. "It's like a fairy-tale land or something, you know? I'm from Louisiana. I've never seen anything like this. But what am I telling you for? You can't even understand me, can you?"

The Korean raised an eyebrow.

"But then it became a nightmare inferno," Donovan added. His eyes began to roll uncontrollably into the back of his head.

Shaking it off, he heard the sound of the Korean moving. Donovan tried to focus and looked up through blurry eyes to see the sniper almost on top of him.

As he approached, the Korean drew his large bayonet from its sheath. The setting sun glinted off of its metal blade as it cleared the leather carrier.

Though he tried to raise his gun, his arm wouldn't work, and Captain Donovan knew this was the end. And strangely, he was at peace with that reality.

Donovan smiled as he caught a glimpse of his brother's watch.

"Still going," he said weakly.

Then he passed out.

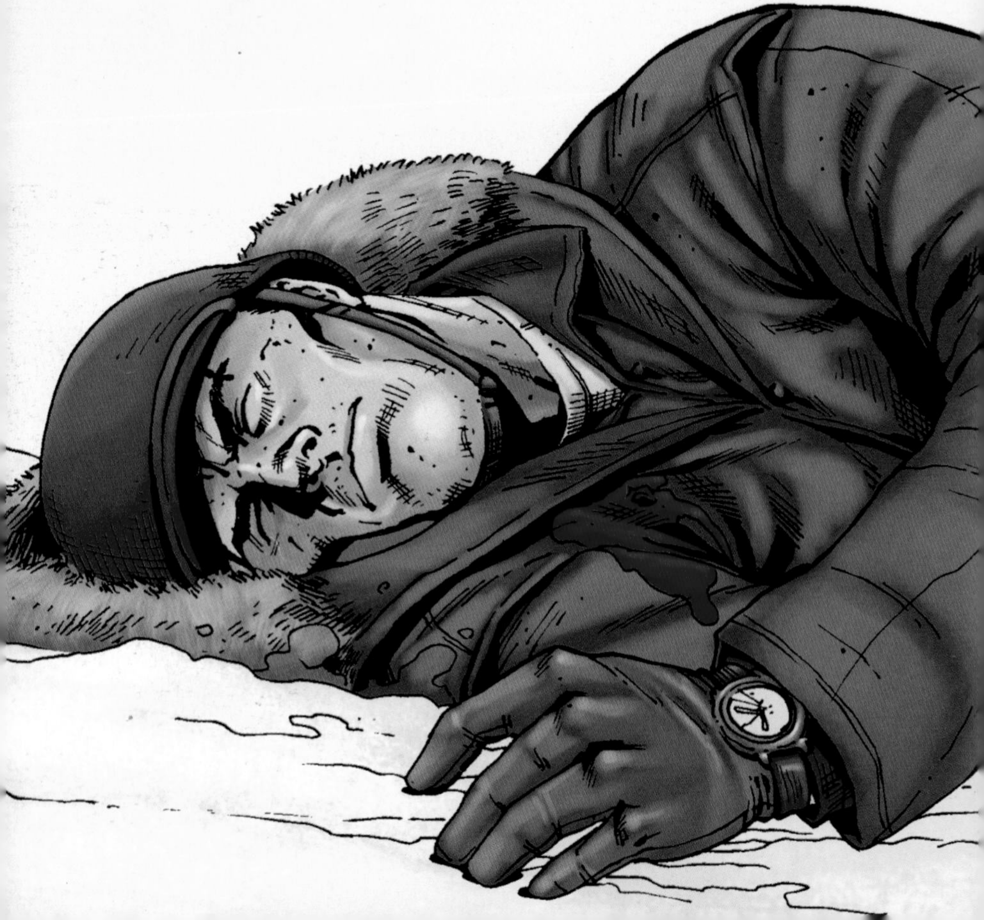

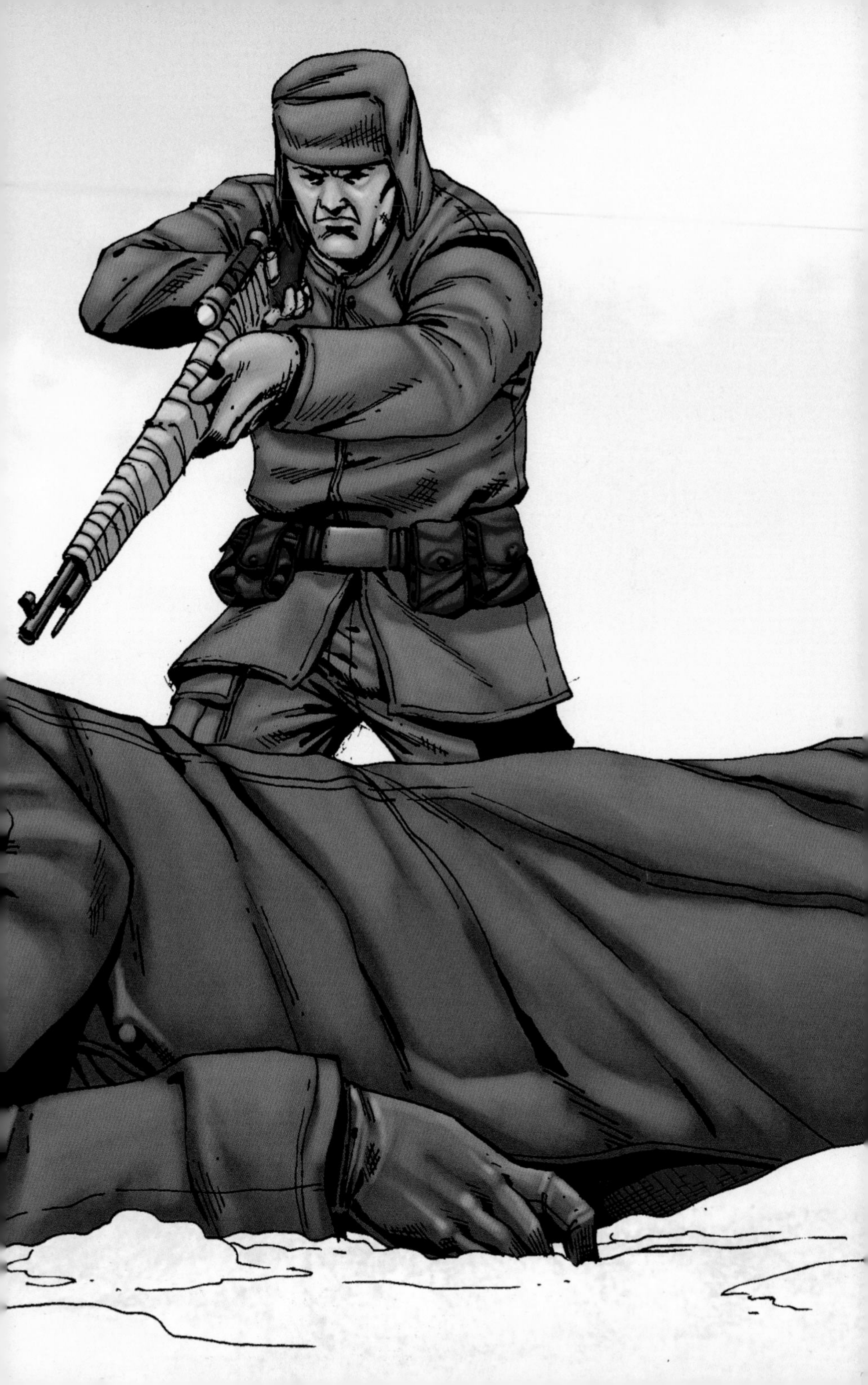

NORTH KOREAN SOLDIERS

HISTORY

In 1950, the North Korean army, also known as the Korean People's Army (KPA) was heavily armed and well trained. During their initial attacks on the south, 100,000 KPA soldiers easily overcame South Korean troops and overtook the city of Seoul. However, as the war continued with U.S. support, the KPA suffered heavy losses. By the end of the Korean War, the KPA had lost more then 290,000 soldiers in less than three years. Today, the KPA remains intact, led by the Supreme Commander Kim Jong-il.

COMMUNISM

North Korea, officially known as the Democratic People's Republic of Korea (DPRK), is a communist country. The government owns all of the land, businesses, and houses, and citizens cannot vote for their leaders. In the United States, leaders are elected by the people, and citizens can buy houses and other items with the money they earn. This type of government is called a democracy. The differences between these views helped lead to the Korean War.

M1911 PISTOL

SPECIFICATIONS

SERVICE: 1911-present
DESIGNER: John M. Browning
WEIGHT: 2.44 pounds
LENGTH: 8.25 inches
BARREL: 5.03 inches
HISTORY: First used by the U.S.
Army on March 29, 1911, the M1911
pistol quickly became a popular
weapon for all branches of the U.S.
military. The single-action, semi-
automatic handgun fired
.45 caliber cartridges from a
seven-round magazine. During
WWII, the U.S. government
purchased 1.9 million M1911s.
They remained a vital weapon
throughout the Korean War.

M9130 RIFLE

A version of the Mosin-Nagant rifle, the
M9130 sniper rifle could fire accurately at
more than 550 yards without optical aid.
More than 37 million were built and used
in Korea, Vietnam, and wars of today.

CHAPTER 003

ISOLATION

Twelve hours earlier . . .

Twenty Marines, each five meters apart, walked along the frozen tundra that was the Toktong Pass. Trees were sparse, and the cover of Mother Nature wasn't as dense as he would've liked. Captain Everett Donovan, 1st Marine Division, 3rd Battalion, 5th Marine Regiment, knew this was an area of operations for the Korean Army and was, unfortunately, where they needed to be.

He and his Counterintelligence Marines had been tasked with a scouting mission. They needed to make sure the coast was clear in this part of Korea so UN and U.S. Forces could advance through the area in the morning.

It appeared they had arrived. Now it was just a matter of looking around and reporting anything suspicious back to their commanders.

Gunnery Sergeant Helmsman, the platoon leader, broke from the others as they stopped and walked over to his commanding officer.

"Your orders, sir?" he asked, continuing to scan the surrounding terrain.

Hills, snow, sparse trees, large boulders, and a total lack of cover meant they were out in the open and could be seen for miles. Helmsman didn't like it.

An older, gruff Marine, Helmsman had been with Donovan in the Pacific during World War II when Donovan was still a first lieutenant. They had history — in combat and out.

On the other side of the Marines, about three miles to the north, lay a small range of mountains that encircled the entire Chosin Basin.

Nodding, Donovan motioned toward the mountains. "The 59th is getting ready to trek through here tomorrow, Gunny," he said. "They're supposed to meet up with the 89th and the 79th. We're all going to meet at on the Chosin Reservoir. If Inchon was the beginning, hopefully, the battle at Chosin will be the ending."

The Gunny shook his head disapprovingly. "Home by Christmas, sir?" he asked.

Smiling, Donovan looked over at the old devil dog. "That upset you, Gunny?" he asked.

"A Marine's place is on the battlefield, not curled up in front of a fireplace like a pussycat, sir," the Gunny barked back at his commanding officer.

Donovan nodded and replied, "I agree."

A light snow began to fall as several of the Marines pulled on gloves and pushed up woolen scarves.

"Not like the Philippines, is it, Gunny?" Donovan said as the snowfall got a bit harder.

"Cold, hot, damp, dry — I don't care, long as my rifle don't freeze shut," Helmsman said, gritting his teeth. "I don't care much about where the fighting's done, as long as I'm the one left standing when it's over."

Helmsman wasn't one for officers. Most of them didn't know their elbows from a Jeep tire, but Donovan was different. The captain listened and cared about his men. And in turn, they respected Donovan.

Helmsman sighed. "It's a bad plan, sir," he said.

Looking over at his gunny, Donovan frowned. "Okay, Gunny, what's eating you?" he asked.

"The Chinese 9th Army is gathering in the towns of Yudami-ni and Sinhung-ni," said Helmsman. "If they push toward Hagaru-ri, they could trap the UN forces on the road between Hagaru-ri and Hungnam."

"Blocking them and the 1st Marines into the Reservoir," added Donovan. "No chance of escape."

"No sir," said Helmsman.

This made Donovan smile. "Then it's a good thing Marines don't retreat, isn't it, Gunny?" he asked.

The Gunnery Sergeant smiled. "Yes, sir, it is indeed."

"Break 'em into their fire teams," said Donovan. "I want a report from each on them. If the 9th Chinese is out there, I want to know about it sooner than later."

A flash of light, a tremendous earth shaking, and instantly, two Marines were killed in an explosion. Secondary explosions rang out as Chinese mortars began raining down on the Marines. They scattered, diving for cover wherever they could.

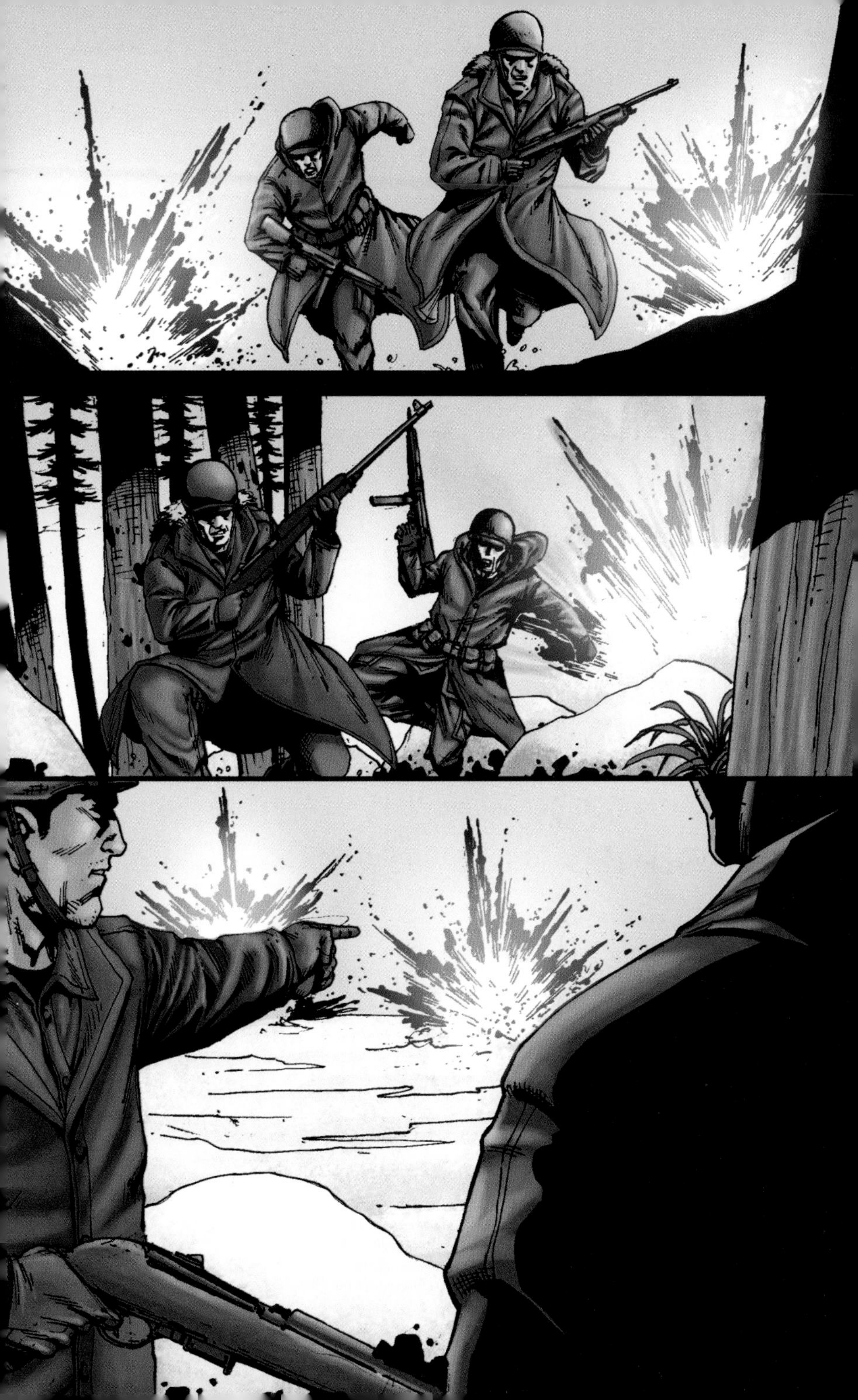

"That soon enough for ya, sir?!" the Gunny scoffed as he racked the action on his M2 rifle and opened fire.

From over the ridgeline to the north, what looked to be about eighty Chinese and North Korean Army soldiers attacked without question or pause.

Expertly, the Marines fired back. Lifeless, Chinese and Korean troops dropped to the dirt. Those who didn't continued to advance as small puffs of smoke appeared in the cliff side.

"INCOMIN'!" Gunny screamed as he reached up and threw the captain under the cover of a nearby boulder.

As Donovan rose, he fired his weapon. In the distance, he saw two Chinese soldiers fall, his aim true. Donovan reached down to help Helmsman up.

"Come on, Gunny, we need to —" he began. But the gunny was dead, having taken most of the explosive force himself to save his captain.

Donovan took pause, shaken, but an old saying ran through his head: *Concentrate on the ones you can save, and mourn the dead later.*

Stick and move, he thought as mortars and rifle fire rained down on them from the entrenched position.

Yelling at his squad leaders, Donovan ordered his men to spread out. "Return fire!" he commanded. "Ya can't hurt 'em if ya don't hit 'em!"

They were outnumbered, and with the Chinese above firing down on them, the Marines wouldn't last long at this location. They needed some air support from the Navy's F9F Panthers and fast.

Ducking and weaving, and with bullets chasing him all the way, Donovan ran to his radio operator.

"Get me —" he began, but Donovan noticed the young radio operator was dead as well. He grabbed the radio handset and turned away from the gruesome sight. Keying the handset, Donovan yelled into it.

"Crossbow 15, this is Cobra 22," he shouted. "I have U.S. casualties — break — we are covered by mortar and small arms fire at two niner romeo."

A series of pops came as Donovan ducked, sparks flying all around him. The radio was completely destroyed in a hail of gunfire.

"No!" he yelled. He threw the handset to the ground and fired at the enemy. Two more Koreans fell.

The Koreans and Chinese pushed forward, their numbers seemingly multiplying.

"They're comin' for us, sir!" one of his Marines screamed over to Donovan with fear in his voice.

"Then at least we know where they are, and they won't get away!" Donovan yelled back. Brass shell casings flipped from his weapon.

His words and his confidence echoed throughout the ranks. He brought a loud "Hoorah" from the men, energized for the fight! The Marines fought hard, but the odds were just too great. Marines crumpled to the deck as Donovan ordered the rest of them to pull back.

One of the Marines was hit square in the chest, and Donovan came to his aid. Placing a hand over the wound, Donovan tried to stop the bleeding, but it came too quickly.

"Corpsman!" Donovan yelled. He looked for the squad's medic, but he was nowhere to be found.

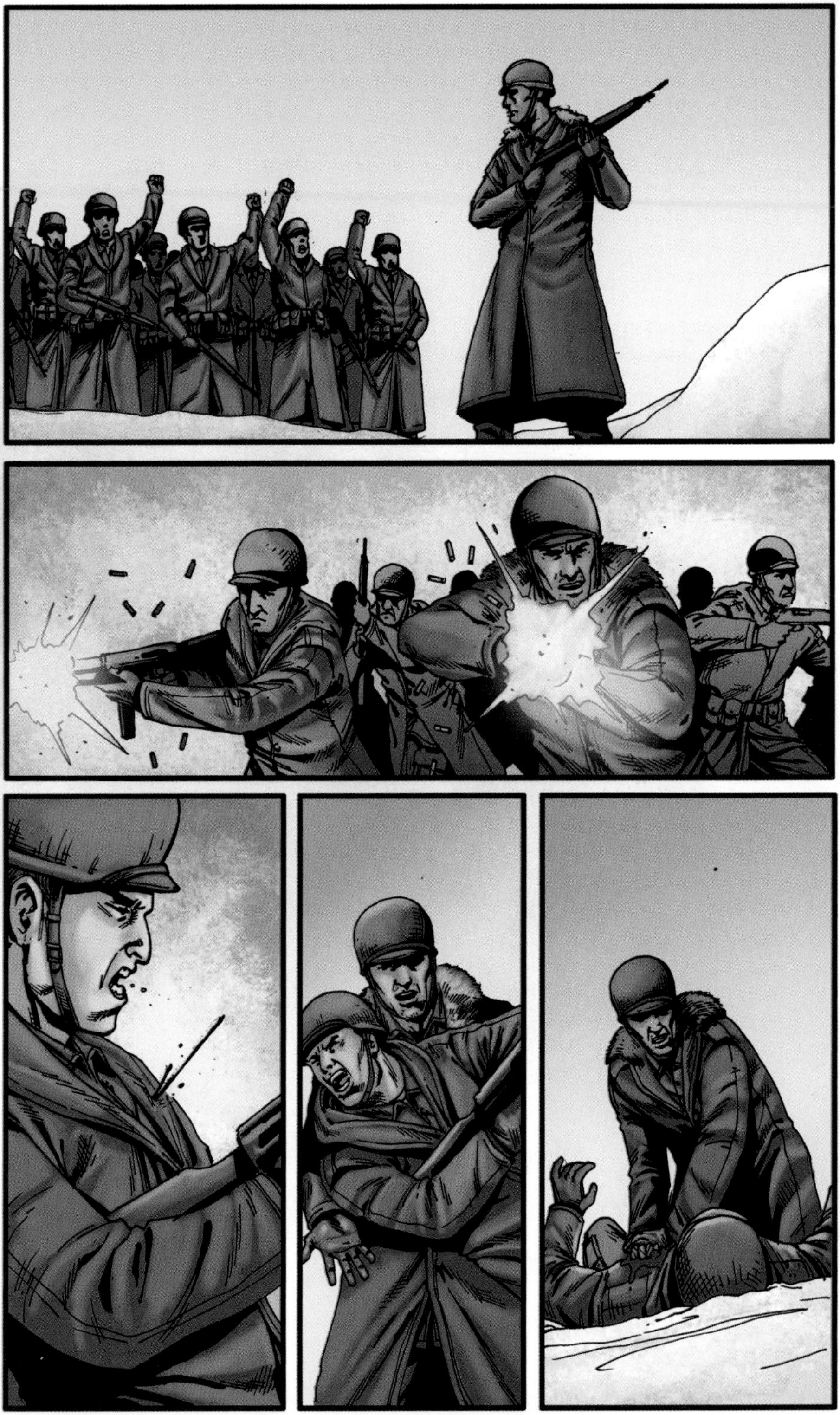

"Don't worry, Sullivan, you'll be outta here soon," Donovan said, grabbing the kid's hand.

But the young Marine knew better. "Sir?" he said. "Please let my pa know . . . I . . . I fought with honor."

Nodding, Donovan agreed, "Like a warrior, son."

And with that, the young Marine was gone. His hand went limp, and Donovan rested it on the young man's chest. Then he picked up his weapon.

Donovan crouched and placed bloody hands next to his mouth, amplifying his words. "Split up and get to Rally Point Alpha!" he commanded the troops.

They divided and began to move in groups. One squad covered the other as they backed out the way they came. But the dropping explosives kept coming, and finally, they completely overwhelmed the Marines.

Looking up, Donovan saw his own fate quickly approaching as a mortar came right for him. He dove out of the way, but the concussion of the explosion blew him through the air. Helmet first, the captain was smashed against a rock and rolled off. His limp body settled in a mortar crater, unconscious.

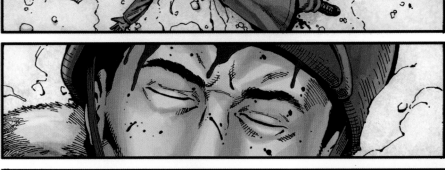

DEBRIEFING

3rd BATTALION, 5th MARINES

SPECIFICATIONS

ALLEGIANCE: United States
BRANCH: U.S. Marine Corps
TYPE: Infantry Battalion
MOTTO: "Get Some"
CONFLICTS:
World War I
World War II
Korean War
Vietnam
Operation Desert Storm
Operation Iraqi Freedom
Operation Phantom Fury

HISTORY

The real-life members of the 3rd
Battalion, 5th Marines have played
a critical role in the U.S. military
since they were first organized on
June 8, 1917. The infantry battalion,
under command of the 5th Marine
Regiment and the 1st Marine
Division, first served during WWI.
Although they've disbanded several
times, this "Get Some" battalion has
been reactivated for every major
U.S. conflict including the Korean
War, where they fought during
the Battle of Pusan Perimeter, the
Battle of Inchon, and the Battle of
Chosin Reservoir.

FACT

The 3rd Battalion, 5th Marines
were nicknamed "Dark Horse."

NAVY F9F PANTHER

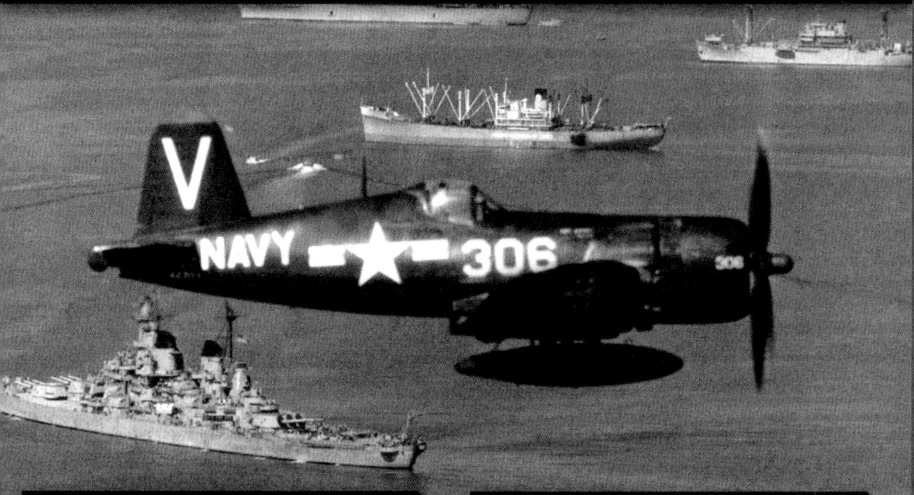
V
NAVY
306

SPECIFICATIONS

FIRST FLIGHT: 11-24-1947
WING SPAN: 38 feet
LENGTH: 37 feet 5 inches
HEIGHT: 11 feet 4 inches
WEIGHT: 9,303 lbs.
MAX SPEED: 575 mph
MAX RANGE: 1,300 miles
CEILING: 44,600 feet
ACCOMMODATION: capable of transporting one crewman (pilot)

FACT

Lieutenant Leonard H. Plog of the U.S. Navy scored the first air-to-air kill of the Korean War.

HISTORY

First built by Grumman Aircraft Engineering Corporation in the late 1940s, the F9F Panther quickly became the most widely used U.S. Navy jet fighter during the Korean War. The F9F Panther was also the first aircraft of the war to score an air-to-air kill, shooting down a North Korean Yak-9 fighter jet on July 3, 1950. With the ability to take off from and land on aircraft carriers and carry 2,000 lbs. of air-to-ground rockets and bombs, the F9F was an effective weapon for the U.S. Navy. By war's end, more than 1,400 had been built.

CHAPTER 004
AWAKENED

Donovan's eyes popped open.

Frantic and scared, he wasn't even sure where he was. The returning memories of the last day still lingered in his mind.

Eyes darting, he observed that night had fallen. A small flickering campfire was burning, lighting up the surrounding trees. As he glanced upward, he saw the Korean sniper standing over him like an angel of death, the bayonet still in his hands.

But now, it was covered in blood.

Panic filled Donovan as he screamed and lashed out like a child. He flailed as he rose, kicking the sniper away from him. Reaching down, Donovan snatched up his .45 pistol, cocked it, and moved forward.

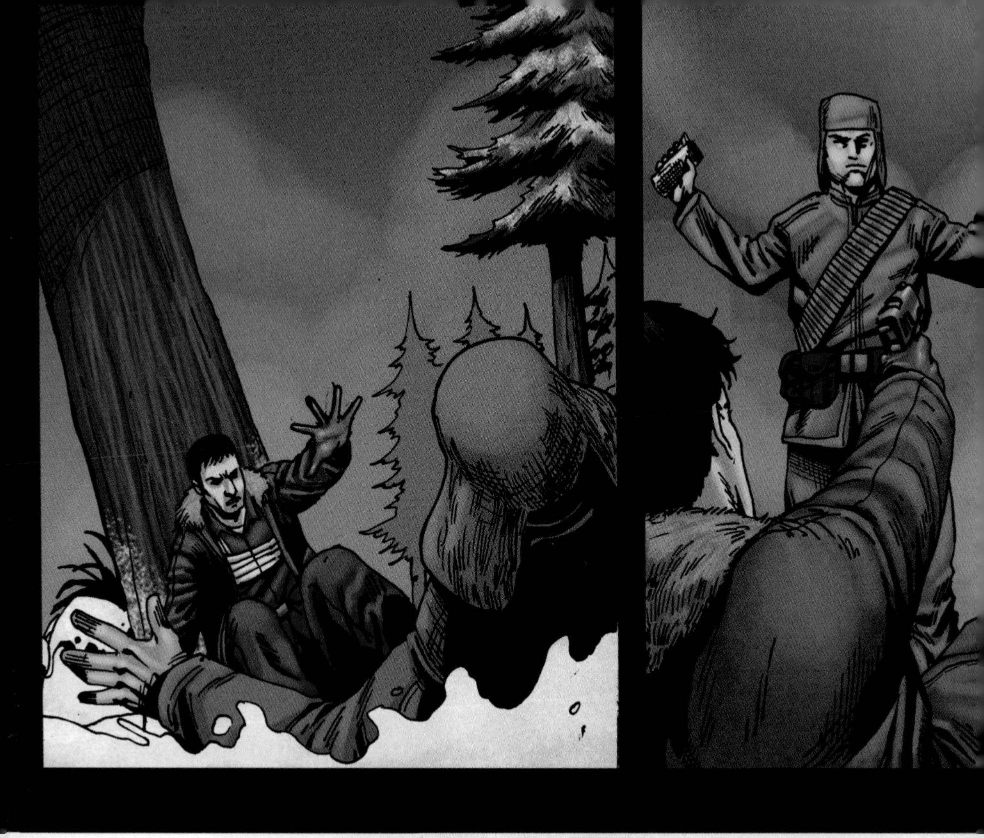

The Korean hit the deck as Donovan came down on him hard, slamming a boot into his chest. Donovan pulled up his .45 and aimed at the Korean's forehead. The sniper dropped his knife and raised his hands.

"*Anio! Anio!*" the Korean pleaded.

As it fell, the knife hit a small metal drinking cup on the ground. The liquid splashed up and onto Donovan's boots, which drew Donovan's attention downward. He breathed heavily, just about to pull the trigger.

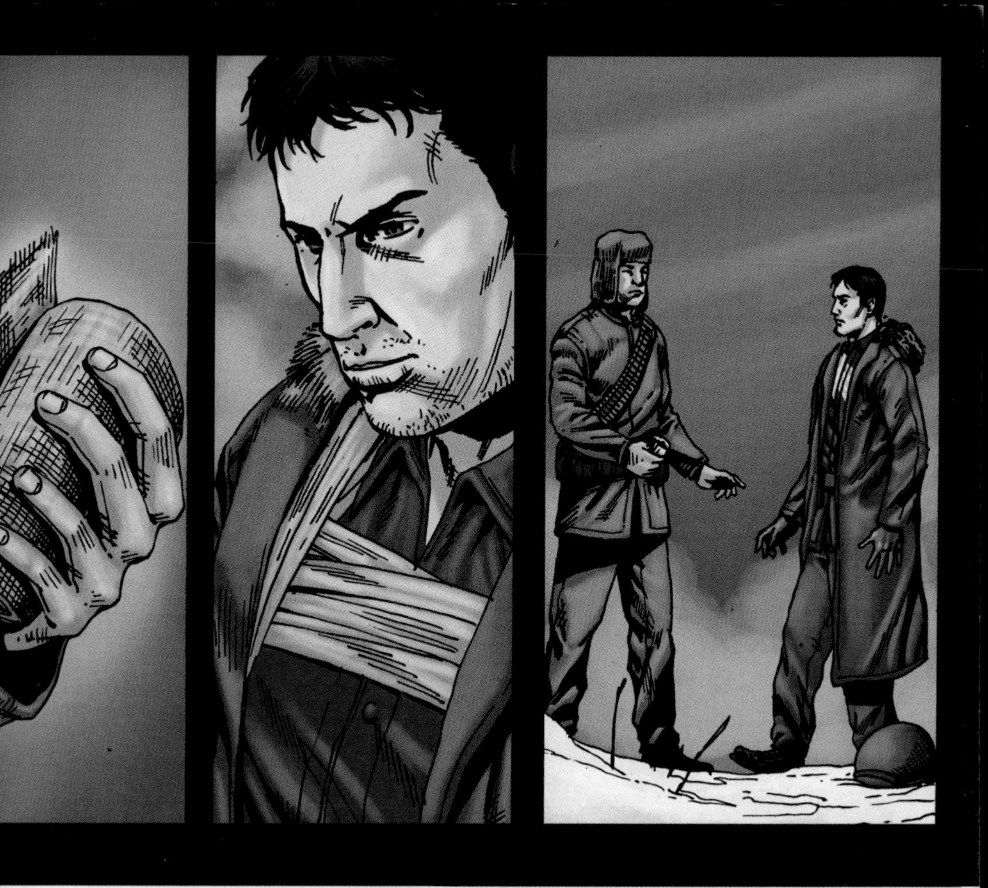

Swirling with the water from the cup was a large amount of blood, but it's what was swimming in the sticky liquid that gave Donovan pause. A small lead ball, mushroomed and misshapen, was covered in a layer of deep red blood.

A bullet.

Donovan looked over at his arm.

A fresh field dressing, white and sterile, had been applied to his shoulder.

The sniper had used his bayonet to dig the slug out and then bandaged him up.

Donovan's head began swimming. Confused, he felt like he was going to pass out. Backing away, Donovan lifted his boot from the sniper's chest, but still covered the Korean with his weapon. He glanced between his shoulder and the defenseless enemy still on the ground, pleading for his life.

At that instant, it hit him.

The Korean had saved his life.

Emotions swirled in Donovan like a massive tornado.

Why?! he wondered.

Why did he do it? Was it a trick? Am I to be taken captive for interrogation?

Or is he genuine?

These questions, coupled with the flashes of returning memories of the previous day's events, finally broke the brave young Marine to his core. He slumped onto the log again.

Tears flooded down his cheeks. Donovan sucked air, letting out small moans as he wept.

He'd seen his share of death and destruction during the Pacific campaign. He'd never see another like it in his lifetime. It was nothing like he'd seen today, not even Iwo Jima.

"They . . . they came at us like a tidal wave," Donovan said. "They didn't stop. And those men . . ."

The captain stopped. His head slightly cocked to the side as his eyes went wide.

" . . . those boys," he corrected himself, "fought like warriors. But we didn't have a chance. When the mortars started pounding us from above, Gunny shoved me under cover. He —" He stopped again. His body trembled uncontrollably.

Very slowly, the Korean sat up, leaned against the log he once sat on, and listened to Donovan cry in the darkness. The small fire reflected off of his face. Donovan's tears glistened in its golden glow. His eyes settled into a distant stare.

"They couldn't move, they were pinned down by rifle fire. We lost two in the first attack," Donovan said. "The looks on their faces. There was nothing I could do. Eighteen Marines, laying there, one on top of another. Crying. Yelling. Burning. And you know what? You know the worst part? What I will never forgive myself for?"

Through the tears, Donovan looked up at the Korean.

"I'm alive, and they're not," he said.

Eyelids shut, Donovan tried to squeeze out the pain. He said softly, "Why? Why didn't you just let me die?"

The sound of sloshing made his eyes open. He saw his canteen before him.

Compassion filled the Korean's eyes. The sniper offered some water to the wounded American.

"Because I make choice. Choice for life. Not just for you," the Korean said softly.

Eyes wide, Donovan looked at him in shock. "You speak English?!" he exclaimed.

The Korean held up his thumb and forefinger. "Little bit," he said, offering up the canteen again.

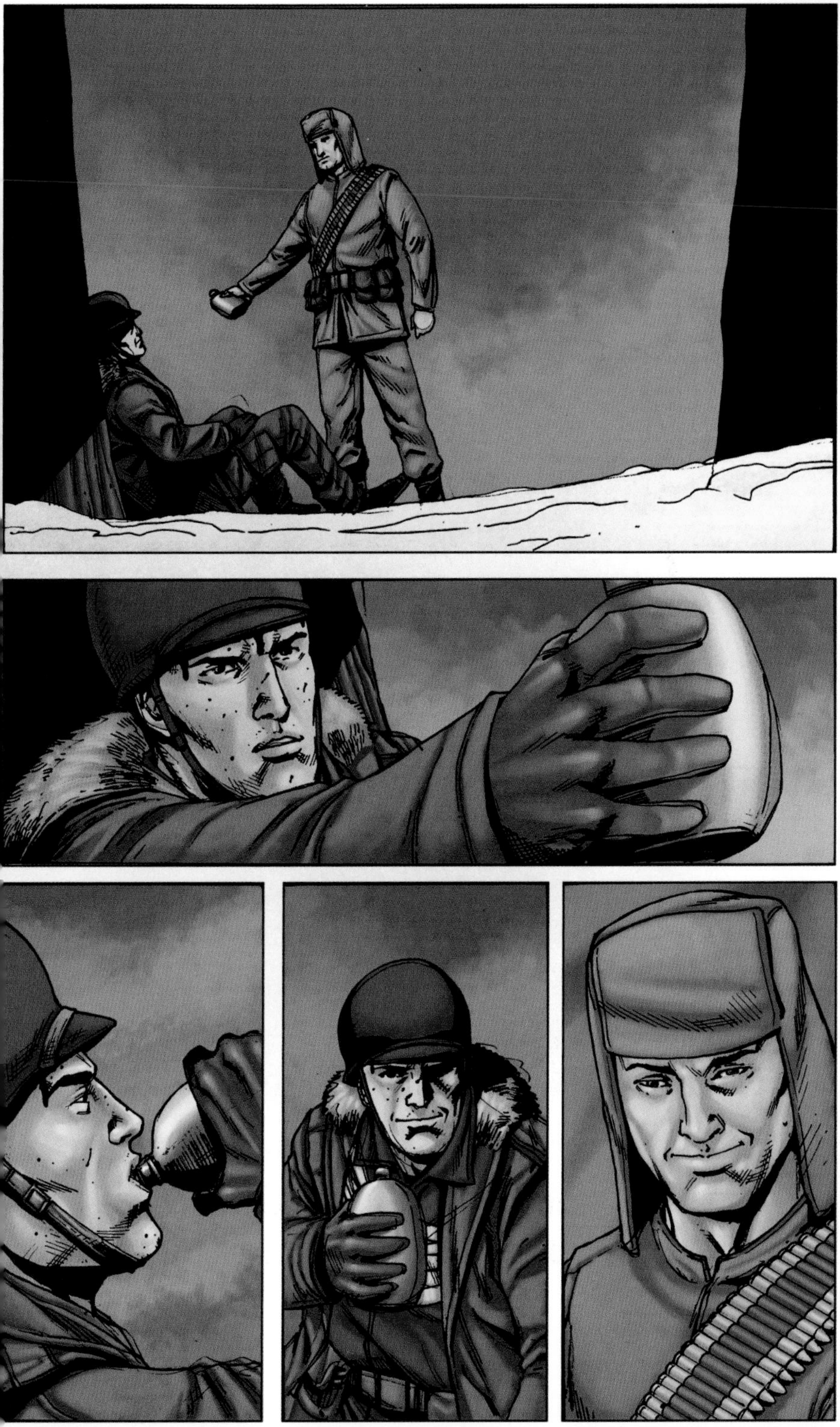

Slowly, Donovan dropped his pistol and took the canteen. He sipped off the top. The swallow went down hard as the water stuck in his scratchy, dry throat. After handing it back, Donovan grinned as the Korean took a sip.

A moment passed. The two men, sworn to kill each other, sat sharing a canteen. In their own little section of the world, the war seemed far behind them.

Quietly, Donovan spoke.

"I don't know why you fixed me up," he said. "I mean, you did shoot me, but maybe it's true. It's easy to kill the faceless enemy, but when you get up close and personal, it changes all the rules."

The Korean stood and walked over to a tree at the far end of the encampment. He leaned against the frozen bark. Looking out into the meadow, the enemy pondered the American, his words, and these last two hours of his life. He understood exactly what the captain was saying.

"Okay, look . . . the way I figure it, we've both got somethin' to get home to. I'm going to back outta here the way I came in," said Donovan as he rose.

"I don't want to kill you," Donovan continued, "and I'm pretty sure I don't want to be dead. So let's just call it a truce and walk away, eh? Sound good?" He outstretched his hand, the gesture of a friendly handshake.

The sniper turned to him, but he suddenly looked angered. A cocked-back hand in the air, he let his fist fly forward like a rocket and clobbered Donovan in the jaw.

THWACK!

The punch sent Donovan reeling to the ground with a resounding thud of flesh and equipment. The Korean stepped over him, retrieved the Colt, and grabbed Donovan by the collar. In an instant, he hoisted Donovan up by the coat and slammed him into a tree. Pistol in the American's face, he angrily barked at him in Korean.

Completely confused by this behavior, Donovan eyed the sniper wildly. Behind him, an entire platoon of thirty Korean soldiers suddenly marched out of the woods, their guns in the air.

The platoon commander walked over to the sniper. The sniper saluted with a head nod, his hands busy holding the American prisoner. This nod signalled that the other man was a commanding officer.

The commander began asking the sniper questions that Donovan, of course, couldn't understand. But he got the gist of the conversation. The sniper punctuated his answers by slamming Donovan against the tree.

Finally the commanding officer smiled and snapped his fingers, and one of the other Koreans stepped forward and handed the sniper an entrenching tool.

Eyes narrowing, the platoon leader looked at the American and waved good-bye. He rallied his troops, and they moved out.

The sniper grabbed Donovan by the collar and led him deeper into the woods, in the opposite direction of the Korean patrol. He yelled the entire time. Gun to his back, Donovan trekked through the trees. The sniper led him by the scruff of the neck.

"So that's it, huh? Orders? I didn't get through to you at all, did I?" Donovan said, continuing his death march.

The Korean sniper was suddenly, and eerily, silent. His face was emotionless, like he was a robot now, the perfect killing machine.

Finally they reached the clearing where he had shot Donovan. After letting go of Donovan's collar, the sniper threw the encased entrenching tool at Donovan's feet. He motioned for Donovan to pick it up.

Angered, Donovan spit on the ground. "No way!" he shouted. "You can kill me if you want, but there is no way I'm diggin' my own grave!"

But the Korean shrugged, confused at Donovan's reaction. He waved at the tool, motioning with the .45 pistol for Donovan to pick up the canvas-cased shovel again. And again, Donovan refused.

Frustrated, the Korean squatted down and grabbed the tool, flipping it over. Another case was attached to its back. This one, a map carrier with compass, was strapped to the entrenching tool. It was a common practice to carry two pieces of equipment as one.

The Korean offered it to Donovan, and the captain slowly began to catch on to what was happening.

The sniper was letting him go.

Pointing at the map, the sniper traced a small path leading back to the Toktong Pass — a better route to where the Americans had been amassing troops.

The sniper pointed to the mountains. "You go!"

As Donovan turned to run, he stopped and reached down into his webbing.

Throwing something to the Korean, he nodded and said, "Here . . ."

Reaching out, the Korean caught Donovan's canteen.

" . . . and thanks," Donovan added.

The Korean smiled and waved him off. "Go!"

Giving a slight salute, the Marine turned and booked it across the clearing.

As he ran, the Korean raised the Colt into the air, taking aim at Donovan's back.

He closed his eyes as he pulled the trigger.

Two shots rang out as the Korean sniper stood, alone in the meadow. His pistol, aimed high, smoked in the cool night air.

He looked out over the clearing to see Captain Donovan, United States Marine Corps, disappearing into the trees.

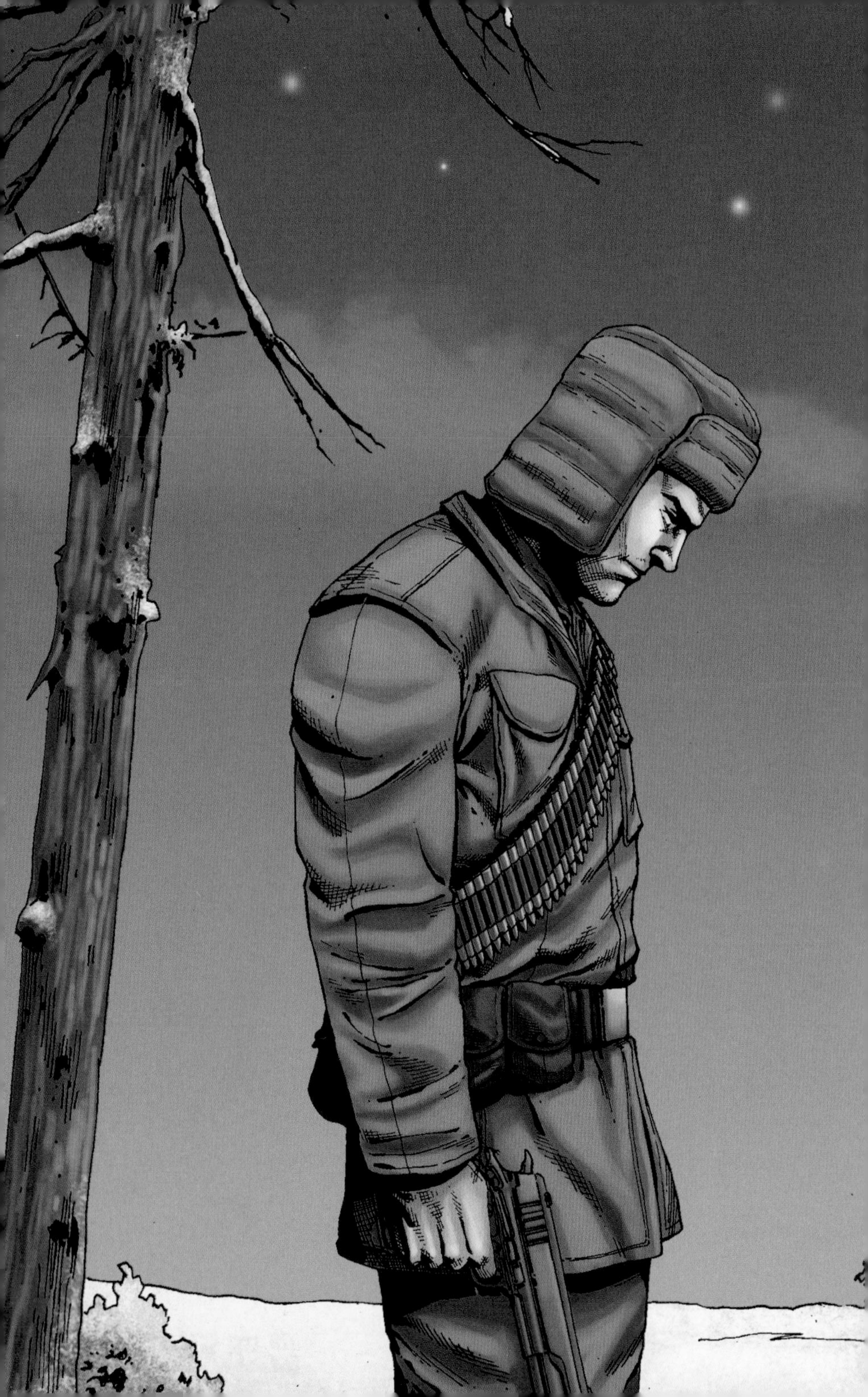

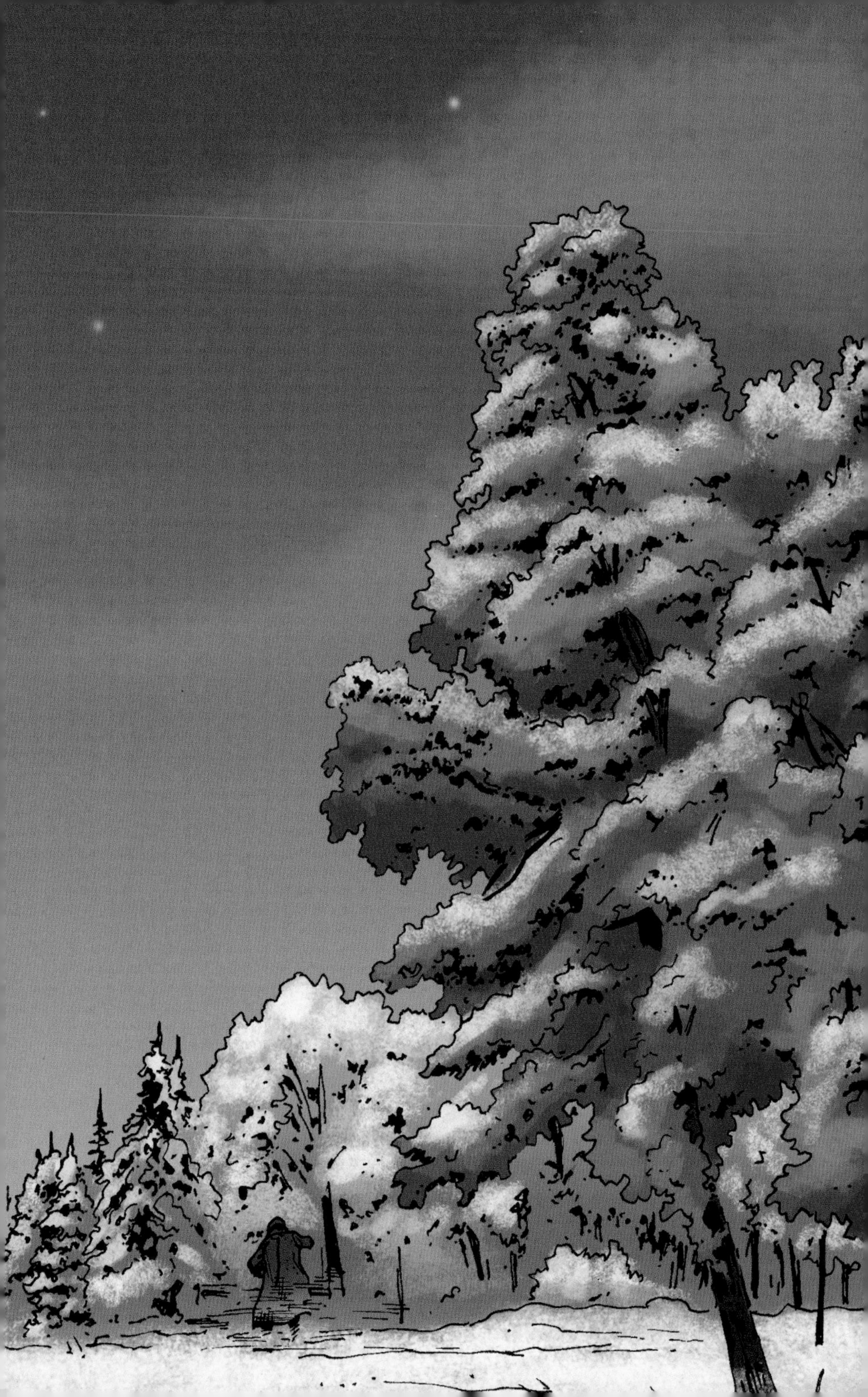

DEBRIEFING

CHOSIN RESERVOIR CAMPAIGN

SPECIFICATIONS

DATES: November 27–December 13, 1950
LOCATION: Chosin Reservoir, North Korea
MILITARY STRENGTH:
United Nations (South Korea, United Kingdom, United States): 30,000 troops
Chinese: 60,000 troops

FACT

The 30,000 UN soldiers who fought during the Battle of Chosin Reservoir in North Korea are often nicknamed the "The Frozen Chosin" or "The Chosin Few."

HISTORY

At the end of 1950, Chinese forces, known as the People's Volunteer Army (PVA), attacked U.S. X Corps soldiers in the northeastern part of North Korea. Soon, 30,000 UN troops were surprised and surrounded by more than double the amount of PVA soldiers. During the next seventeen days, UN soldiers (which included troops from South Korea, the United Kingdom, and the United States) endured harsh conditions and fought their way out of the trap. In the process, the UN was forced out of North Korea. However, the brutal battle left the Chinese forces crippled.

DEADLY CONDITIONS

HISTORY

One of the deadliest forces facing soldiers during the Korean War wasn't enemy troops; it was the weather. More than 6 million troops, or 90% of the soldiers serving during the war, suffered some form of frostbite. Those who fought in the Battle of Chosin Reservoir were particularly hard hit. Temperatures in the mountains of North Korea dipped to less than 30 degrees below zero during the battle. With inadequate gear, thousands lost fingers and toes to the subzero temps; many others lost their lives.

COLD GEAR

At the beginning of the Korean War, U.S. soldiers wore similar uniforms to those worn in World War II. However, after suffering injuries and losses to frostbite during the first winter in North Korea, the military adopted cold weather gear. These items included the M1951 Parka, Mitten Shells, Trouser Shells, and the M1951 Winter Pile Hat. They also added insulated boots, which soldiers dubbed "Mickey Mouse Boots," for their extra large size.

CHAPTER 005

THE COST OF WAR

Flakes of white began to fall as the sniper made his way back into his camp. Exiting the cover of the trees, he nodded hellos to the guards who recognized him as he made for his tent. His instrument of death hung from his arm, slung over his shoulder. The American's canteen was tucked secretly into his shirt.

The night was especially cold, even for a Korean winter, and several of the soldiers had lit fires in fifty-gallon drums. The flames licked at the biting wind. Soldiers stood in packs, warming themselves over the fire as the sniper approached.

His comrades welcomed him back to camp, calling him a hero to the people for what he had done to the Marine. Of course, he played along. He knew a firing squad would be his fate if what he had done was even suspected by any of the others.

As he warmed his cold hands over the fire, his commanding officer slapped him on the back.

"Excellent work, Jung-woo!" he said, smiling from ear to ear.

The sniper bowed his head, not making eye contact with his commander. "Thank you, sir," he replied.

"Come! All of you!" the commander said, waving everyone to follow.

"It has been a long day and much has changed since you were on your patrols," he said as he entered the tent.

Inside was dark, lit only by the five red-lens lanterns that sat on the work spaces edging the walls of the tent.

This was the platoon's operations center.

Plastic-covered maps hung on the walls and various pieces of communications equipment flanked the large table in the center of the space. On it sat an image of the entire Chosin Reservoir, with several locations circled in red.

"Because of the American attack today, we doubled our mine-placing efforts!" said the commander.

"I am happy to announce the entire Toktong Pass has been fortified with a defensive perimeter that not even a foot soldier could pass through!" he shouted.

Confused, the sniper eyed the map. That was exactly the area he had sent the American into, not ten minutes earlier.

"In the morning, the PVA 20th and 27th Corps will launch multiple attacks and ambushes along the road between the Chosin Reservoir and Koto-ri. We will be a part of that attack," the commander said proudly.

The soldiers cheered and waved fists in the air. The chance to strike against the invading Americans made them all proud to be fighting for what they believed in. All but the sniper.

Sadly, the sniper left the celebrating soldiers behind as he quietly snuck out of the tent. The bitter cold slapped his face as he walked alone, the cheers of the men fading out behind him.

He stopped as he came to the edge of the trees, and leaned against one of them. Above, the moon was full. Its glowing face stared back at him.

The sniper mouthed a quiet prayer for the American he had unknowingly put into harm's way. The sudden sound of snow crunching behind him made him turn.

"What's the matter, Jung-woo?" the commander asked as he approached the sniper.

The sniper sighed. "Tomorrow will be the beginning of a bloodbath, sir . . ." he said, continuing to gaze at the moon with concern.

The commander smiled. "Yes," he said. "And it will be the beginning of a glorious victory for the North."

"Even a single dead man is anything but glorious," the sniper replied. "It's wisdom, compassion, and courage that are the moral qualities of men."

"Bah!" the commander said. "Morals are righteous anecdotes written by the victors of conflict. We must fight to protect our way of life — to continue as a unified people — or all will be lost. The politics of this war are very hard to understand."

"Confucius tells us life is very simple, sir, but it is we who insist on making it complicated," the sniper said.

The commander put a hand on the sniper's shoulder. "Confucius understood what it was to be a soldier," he said. "We truly appreciate life, because only soldiers know how quickly it could be taken away."

The sniper nodded. "But Confucius wasn't a soldier, and nothing in today's world is simple," he replied.

"Then why? Why do we do these immoral things? Murder people over land, or a different way of thinking than our own?" he asked softly.

"Because we're soldiers and when you're a soldier, it isn't murder, it's your duty. All war is immoral but if you let that bother you, you're not a good soldier," he replied.

The words hung on the breeze as they stood looking at the moon.

Finally, the commander looked at his sniper. "We've known one another for a very long time, Jung-woo. What's really troubling you?"

"It's . . ." stopping, Jung-woo looked at the ground and chuckled a bit. "It's complicated."

"How could you complicate your life?" he asked.

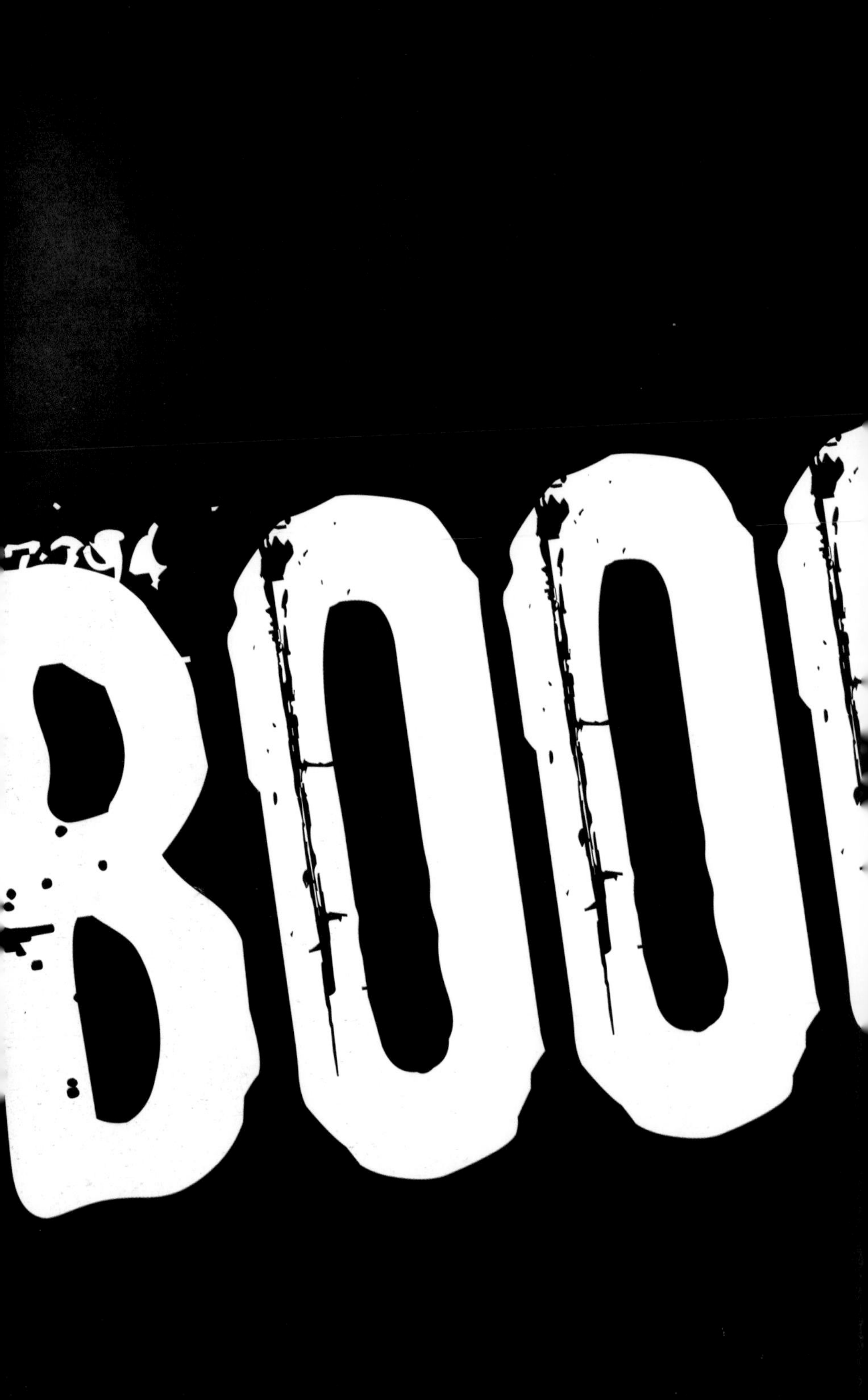
BOOO

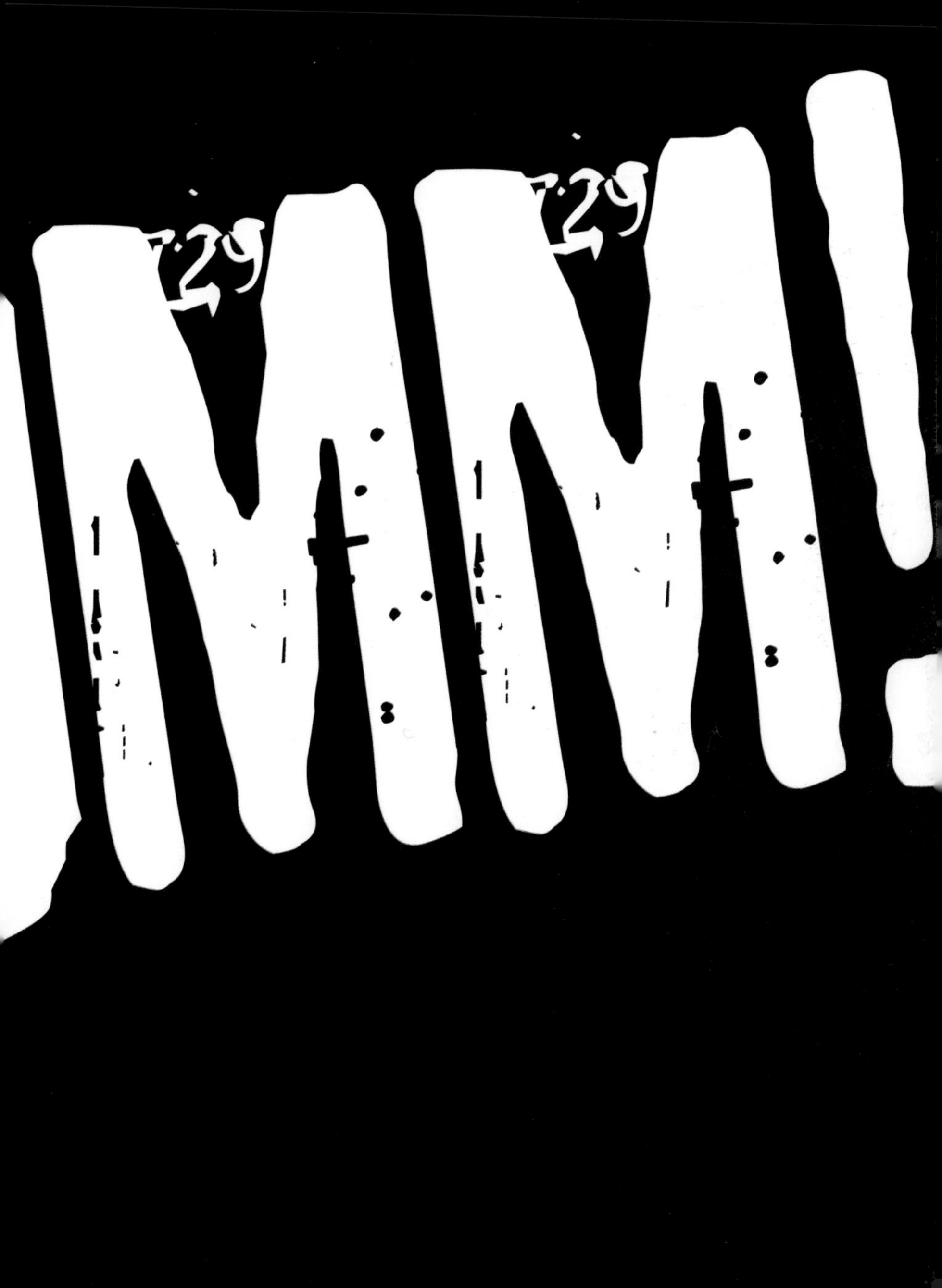
MM!

The distinct sound of an exploding mine rang out in the distance.

Puzzled, the commander's gaze shot up to the horizon. He saw the small puff of gray smoke, backlit by the heavenly glow of the moon, rolling into the air.

The commander glanced from the smoke to his man and back again. But all became immediately clear as the Korean sniper removed Donovan's canteen from his belt and offered it to the commander.

"Drink, sir?" the sniper asked.

Eyes narrowing, the commander took the sniper by the arm.

"Traitor!" he said angrily as he knocked the canteen out of his hand. The water spilled out, pooling up on the ground.

"Guards!" the commander yelled.

Behind them, two armed soldiers appeared and took the sniper into custody.

"You will pay for what you have done!" the commander yelled.

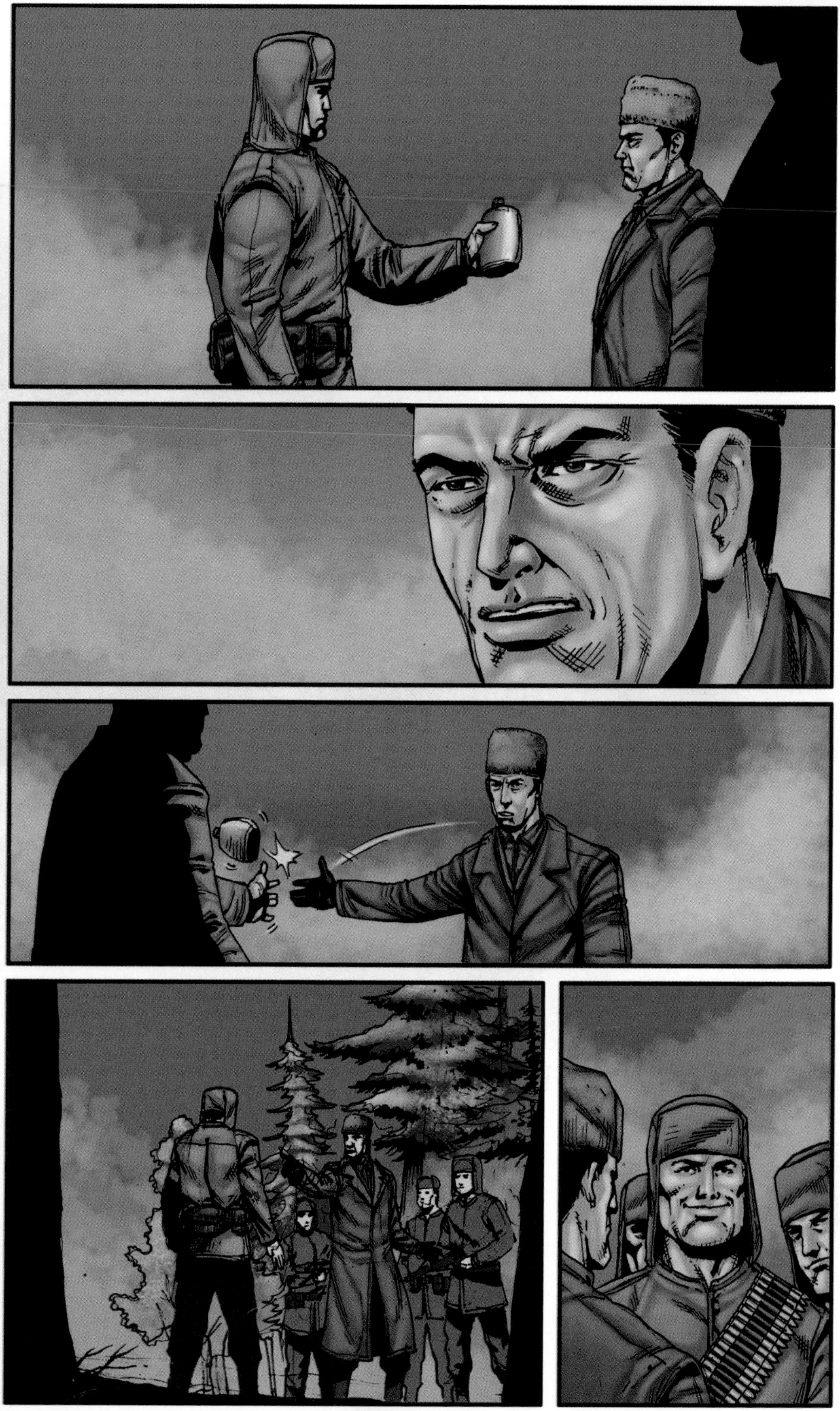

The sniper cocked an eyebrow at his commanding officer, tears welling up in his eyes.

"We all will, sir. But that debt will not be settled by man," he said. Then as the guards dragged him away, the commander looking on in awe.

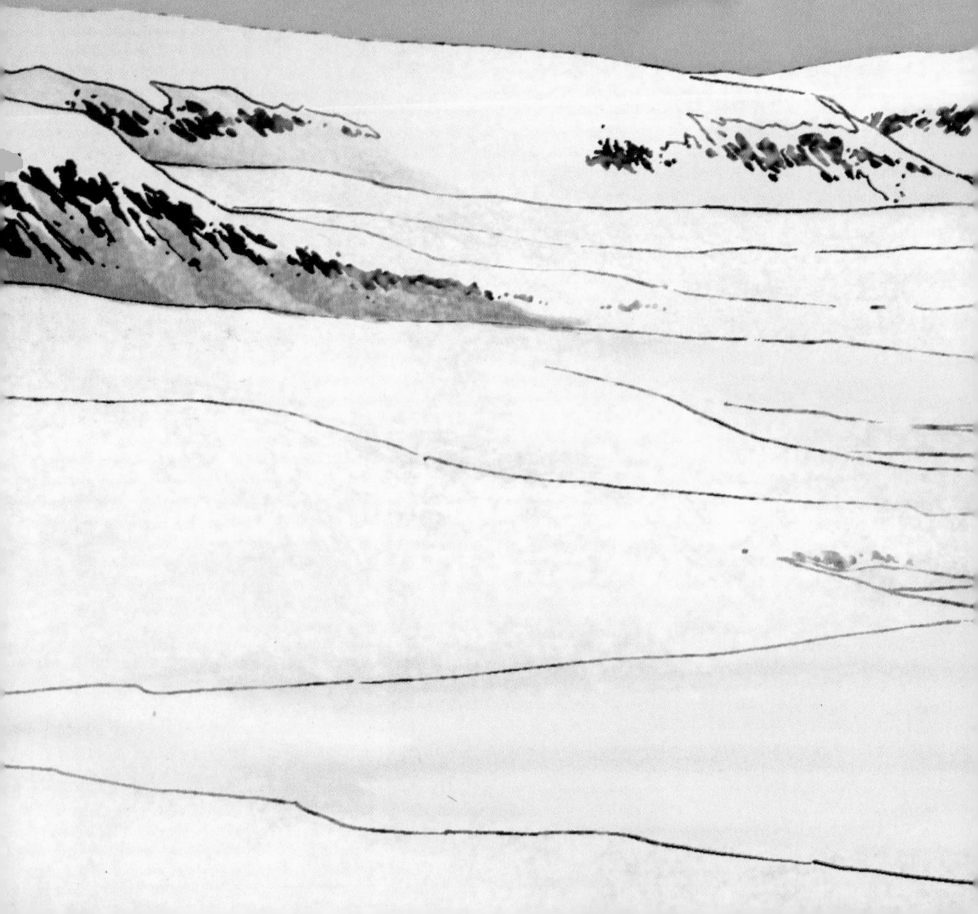

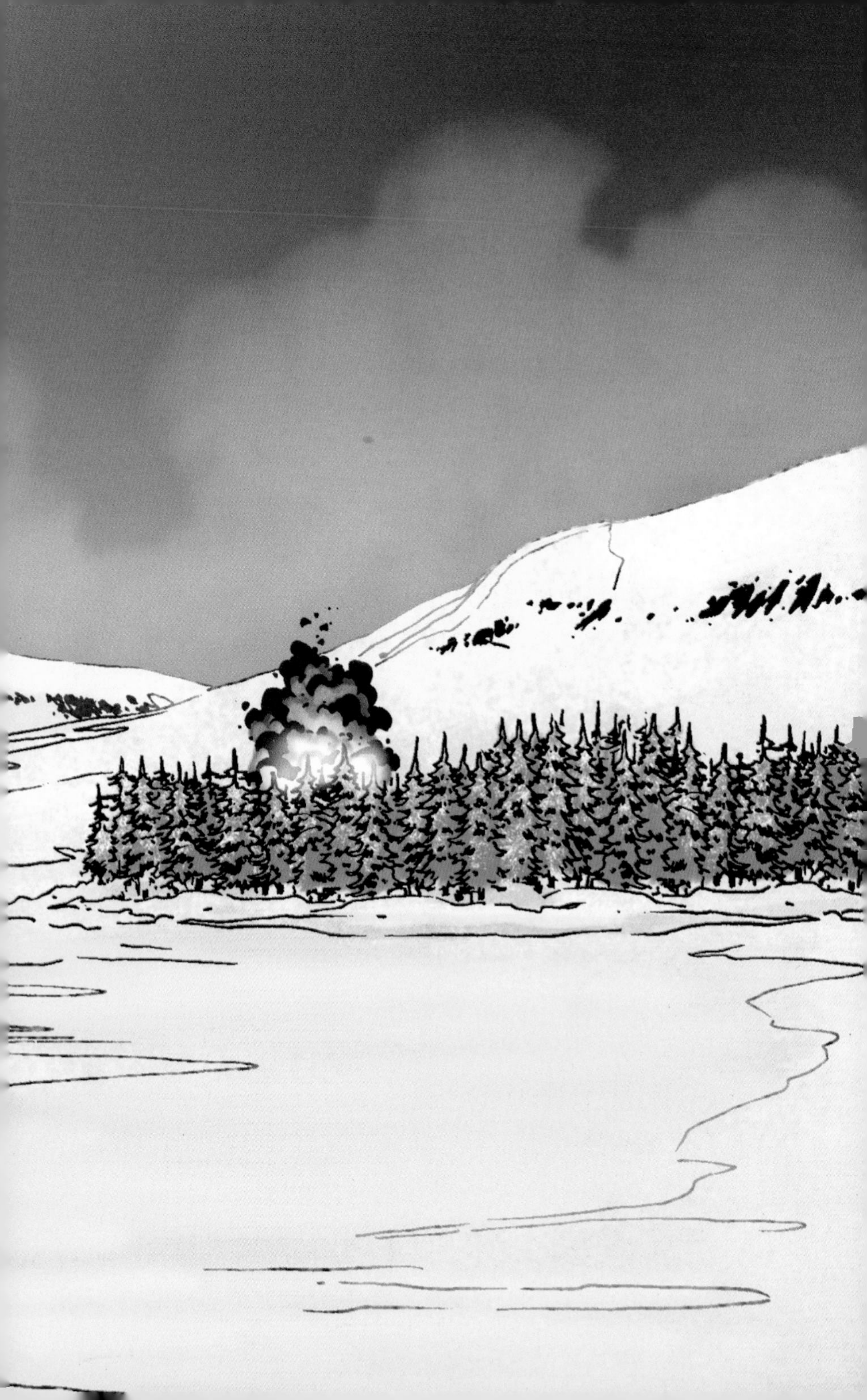

DEBRIEFING

CASUALTIES OF THE KOREAN WAR

STATISTICS

Casualty statistics vary widely. However, many soldiers paid the ultimate price during the Korean War. Below are some historical estimates:

COUNTRY	TOTAL DEATHS
China	100,000-900,000
North Korea	520,000
South Korea	420,000
UN Allies	16,0000
United States	36,940

WAR MEMORIAL

Dedicated on July 27, 1995, the Korean War Veterans Memorial in Washington, D.C., honors those who fought and died in the Korean War. Operated by the National Park Service, the memorial features a 164-foot long granite wall, etched with the photos of 2,500 U.S. troops. The memorial also features 19 stainless steel statues, each standing 7 feet 3 inches tall. These statues commemorate a squad on patrol and represent members from each branch of the Armed Forces. More than 3 million people visit each year.

SURRENDER

HISTORY

Although negotiations for a cease fire began on July 10, 1951, fighting on the Korean Peninsula continued for two more years. Finally, on July 27, 1953, all sides agreed to end the conflict. As part of the agreement, the parties formed a middle ground called Korean Demilitarized Zone (DMZ). Running along the 38th parallel, this 160-mile long border area still separates the two countries. It is nearly 2.5 miles wide and monitored by armed guard on both sides. The buffer zone also includes a Joint Security Area, used for negotiations since 1953.

AFTERMATH

Today, the DMZ still divides the Korean Peninsula. South Korea, officially known as Republic of Korea, remains an independent nation with a democratic republic system of government, which is similar to the U.S. government. North Korea, or Democratic People's Republic of Korea, remains a communist country. It is led by Kim Jong Il, the son of Kim Il Sung. U.S. leaders believe Kim Jon Il and the Korean People's Army remain a threat and continue to provide security in South Korea.

EXTRAS

THE DONOVAN FAMILY

Like many real-life soldiers, the Donovan family has a history of military service. Trace their courage, tradition, and loyalty through the ages, and read other stories of these American heroes.

Renee Woodsworth
1925-1988

Michael Donovan
1926-1979

Military Rank: PFC
World War II
featured in *A Time for War*

Robert Donovan
1907-1956

Richard Lemke
1933-2001

Lillian Garvey
1905-1941

Mary Ann Donovan
1929-1988

Marcy Jacobson
1918-1941

Everett Donovan
1932-1951

Military Rank: CAPT
Korean War
featured in *Blood Brotherhood*

John Donovan
1946-2010

Harriet Winslow
1949-present

Tamara Donovan
1948-1965

Steven Donovan
1952-present

Terry Donovan
1971-present

Elizabeth Jackson
1973-present

Robert Donovan
1976-present

Katherine Donovan
1980-present

Michael Lemke
1954-present

Jacqueline Kriesel
1954-present

Donald Lemke
1978-present

Amy Jordan
1984-present

Verner Donovan
1951-present

Military Rank: LT
War in Vietnam
featured in *Fighting Phantoms*

Jenny Dahl
1953-2004

Lester Donovan
1972-present

Military Rank: LCDR
War in Afghanistan
featured in *Control Under Fire*

EXTRAS

ABOUT THE AUTHOR

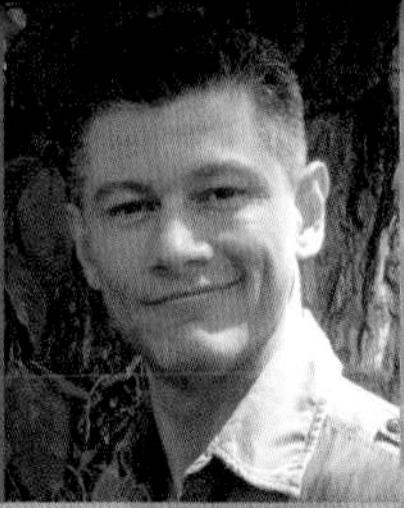

M. ZACHARY SHERMAN is a veteran of the United States Marine Corps. He has written comics for Marvel, Radical, Image, and Dark Horse. His recent work includes *America's Army: The Graphic Novel, Earp: Saint for Sinners*, and the second book in the SOCOM: SEAL Team Seven trilogy.

AUTHOR Q&A

Q: Any relation to the Civil War Union General William Tecumseh Sherman?

A: Yes, indeed! I was one of the only members of my family lineage to not have some kind of active duty military participation — until I joined the U.S. Marines at age 28.

Q: Why did you decide to join the U.S. Marine Corps? How did the experience change you?

A: I had been working at the same job for a while when I thought I needed to start giving back. The biggest change for me was the ability to see something greater than myself; I got a real sense of the world going on outside of just my immediate, selfish surroundings. The Marines helped me to grow up a lot. They taught me the focus and discipline that helped get me where I am today.

Q: When did you decide to become a writer?

A: I've been writing all my life, but the first professional gig I ever had was a screenplay for Illya Salkind (*Superman* 1-3) back in 1995. But it was a secondary profession, with small assignments here and there, and it wasn't until around 2005 that I began to get serious.

Q: Has your military experience affected your writing?

A: Absolutely, especially the discipline I have obtained. Time management is key when working on projects, so you must be able to govern yourself. In regards to story, I've met and been with many different people, which enabled me to become a better storyteller through character.

Q: Describe your approach to the Bloodlines series. Did personal experiences in the military influence the stories?

A: Yes and no. I didn't have these types of experiences in the military, but the characters are based on real people I've encountered. And those scenarios are all real, just the characters we follow have been inserted into the time lines. I wanted the stories to fit into real history, real battles, but have characters we may not have heard of be the focus of those stories. I've tried to retell the truth of the battle with a small change in the players.

Q: Any future plans for the Bloodlines series?

A: There are so many battles through history that people don't know about. If they hadn't happened, the world would be a much different place! It's important to hear about these events. If we can learn from history, we can sidestep the mistakes we've made as we move forward.

ABOUT THE ILLUSTRATOR

FRITZ CASAS is a freelance illustrator for the internationally renowned creative studio Glass House Graphics, Inc. He lives in Manila, Philippines, where he enjoys watching movies, gaming, and playing his guitar.

A CALL TO ACTION

WORLD WAR II

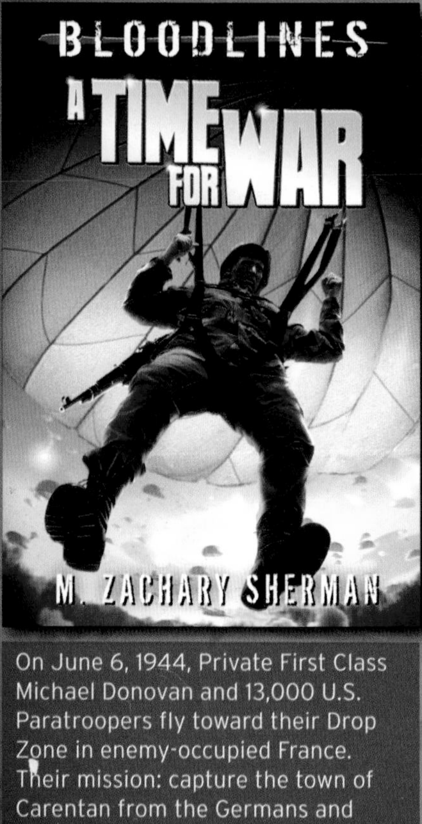
BLOODLINES
A TIME FOR WAR
M. ZACHARY SHERMAN

On June 6, 1944, Private First Class Michael Donovan and 13,000 U.S. Paratroopers fly toward their Drop Zone in enemy-occupied France. Their mission: capture the town of Carentan from the Germans and secure an operations base for Allied forces. Suddenly, the sky explodes, and their C-47 Skytrain is hit with anti-aircraft fire! Within moments, the troops exit the plane and plummet toward a deadly destination. On the ground, Donovan finds himself alone in the lion's den without a weapon. In order to survive, the rookie soldier must rely on his instincts and locate his platoon before time runs out.

KOREAN WAR

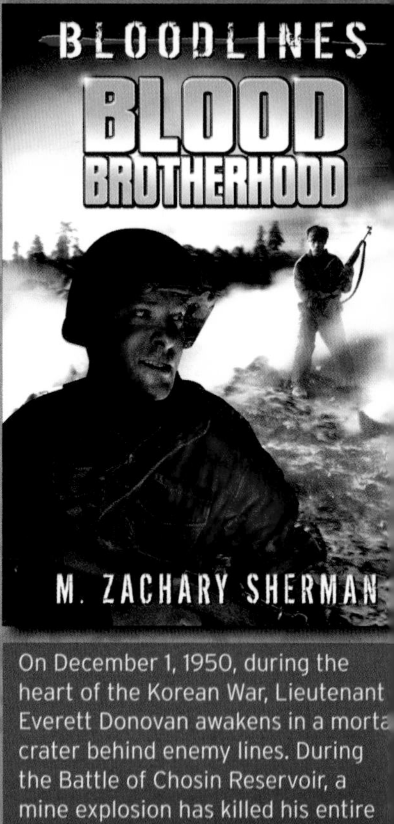
BLOODLINES
BLOOD BROTHERHOOD
M. ZACHARY SHERMAN

On December 1, 1950, during the heart of the Korean War, Lieutenant Everett Donovan awakens in a morta crater behind enemy lines. During the Battle of Chosin Reservoir, a mine explosion has killed his entire platoon of U.S. Marines. Shaken and shivering from the subzero temps, the lieutenant struggles to his feet and stands among the bodies of his fellow Devil Dogs. Suddenly, a shot rings out! Donovan falls to his knees and when he looks up, he's face to face with his Korean counterpart. Both men know the standoff will end in brotherhood or blood — and neither choice will come easily.

VIETNAM WAR

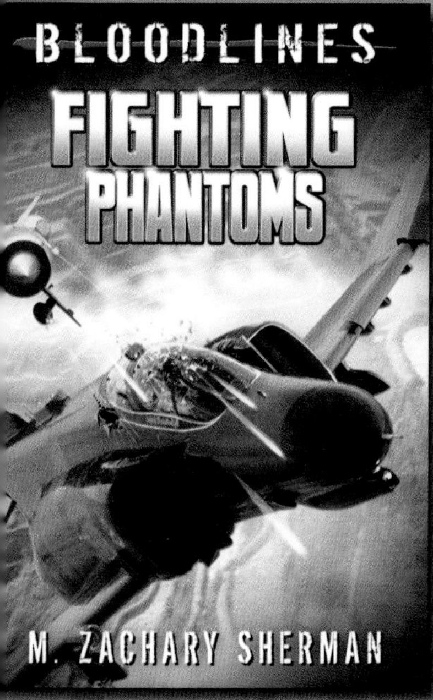

BLOODLINES
FIGHTING PHANTOMS

M. ZACHARY SHERMAN

AFGHANISTAN

BLOODLINES
CONTROL *UNDER* FIRE

M. ZACHARY SHERMAN

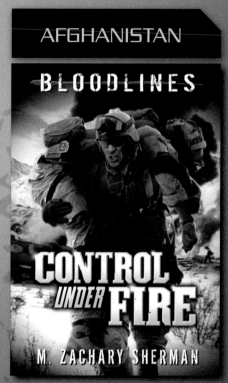

late 1970, Lieutenant Verner
onovan sits aboard an aircraft
arrier, waiting to fly his F-4 Phantom
over Vietnam. He's the lead roll for
e next hop and eager to help the
S. troops on the ground. Suddenly,
e call comes in – a Marine
nit requires air support! Within
oments, Donovan and other pilots
e in their birds and into the skies.
oon, however, a dogfight with MiG
ghter planes takes a turn for the
orse, and the lieutenant ejects over
nemy territory. His copilot is injured
the fall, and Donovan must make a
fficult decision: to save his friend,
e must first leave him behind.

Technology and air superiority
equals success in modern warfare.
But even during the War in
Afghanistan, satellite recon and
smart bombs cannot replace soldiers
on the ground. When a SEAL team
Seahawk helicopter goes down in
the icy mountains of Kandahar,
Lieutenant Lester Donovan must
make a difficult decision: follow
orders or go "off mission" and save
his fellow soldiers. With Taliban
terrorists at every turn, neither
decision will be easy. He'll need
his instincts and some high-tech
weaponry to get off of the hillside
and back to base alive!

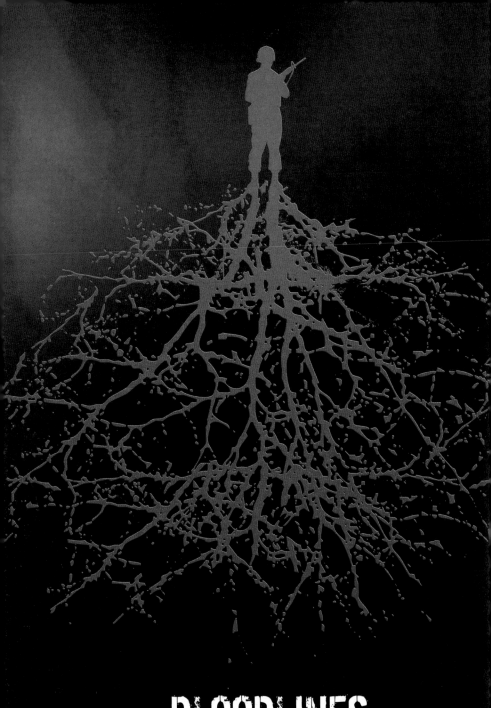

BLOODLINES

www.capstonepub.com

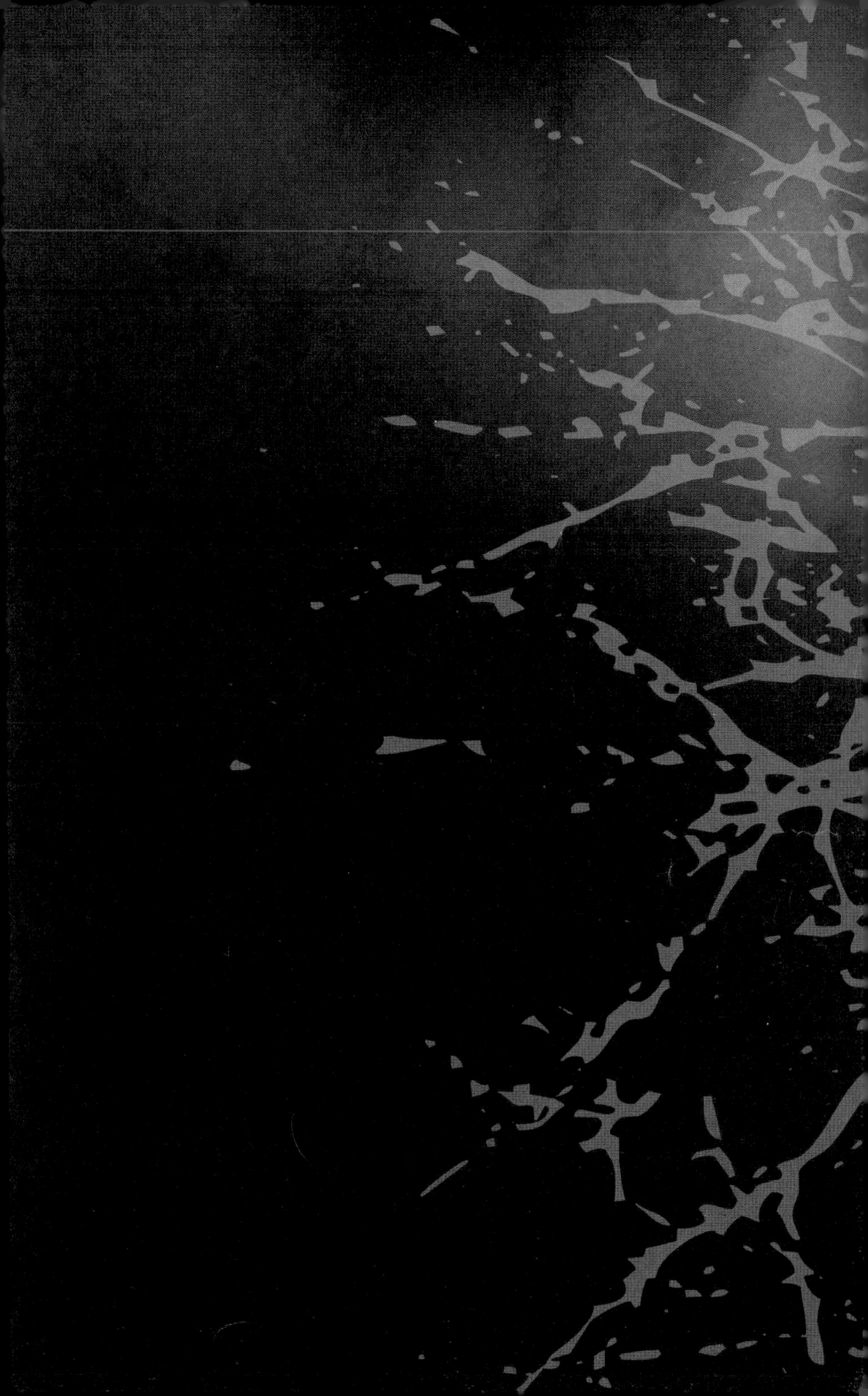

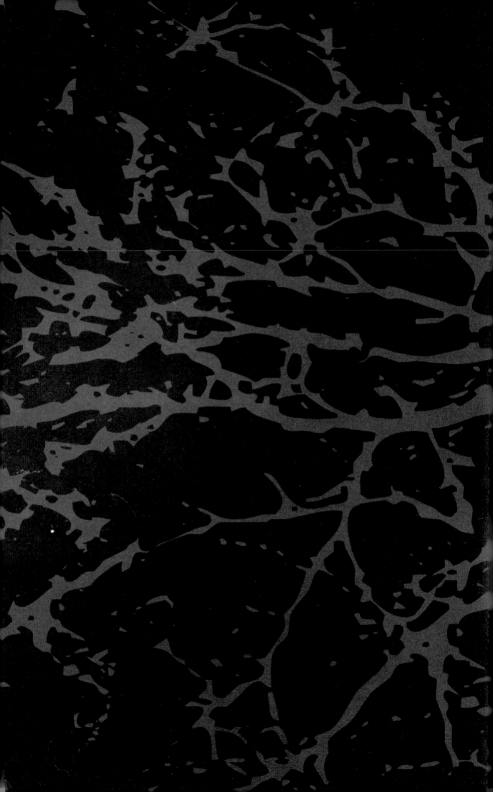

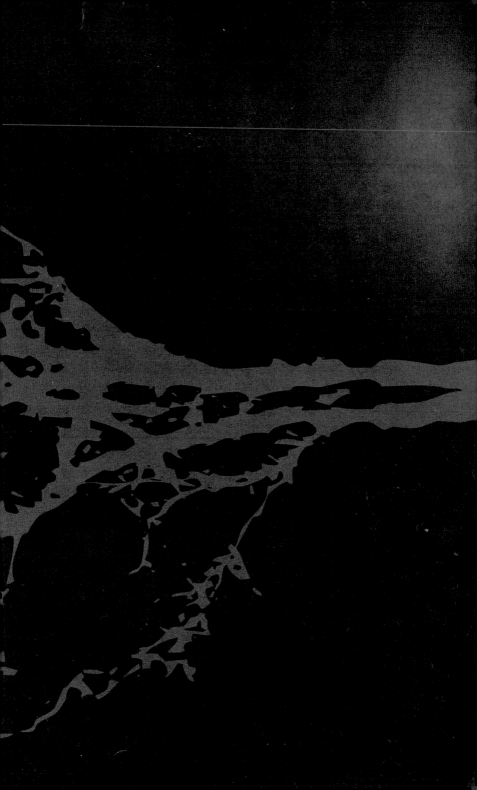

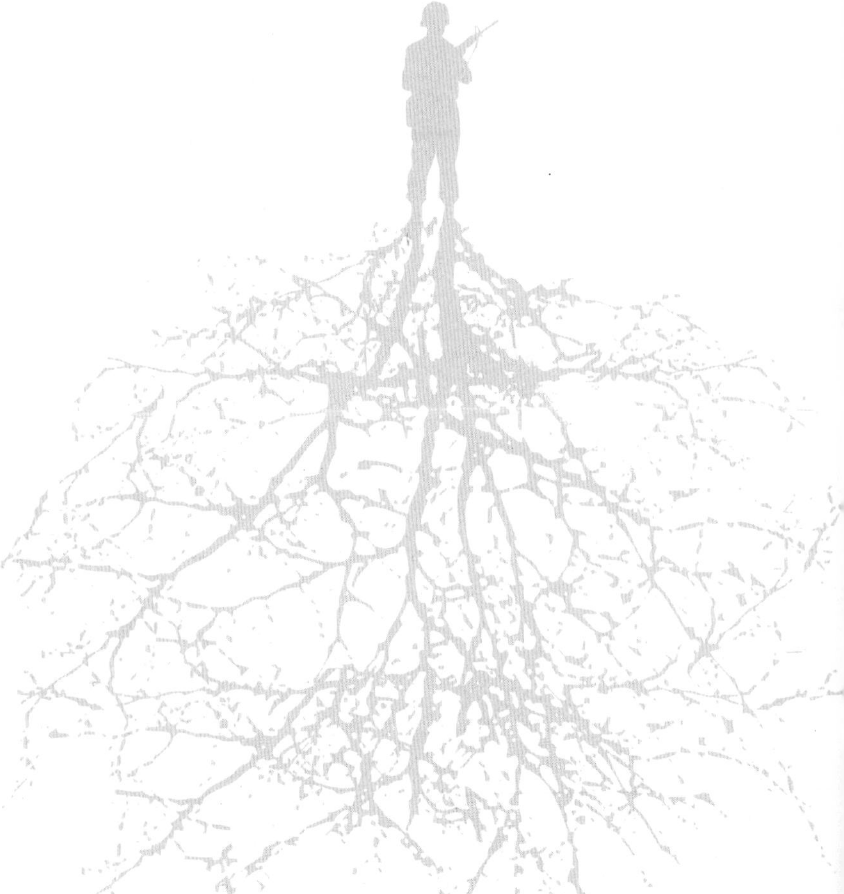